Colby had to fight to keep his touch gentle

Desire dug its claws into him. He wanted...damn, how fiercely he wanted to pull her into his arms and kiss her until the regret of the past and the question mark of the future both disappeared into the fire of right now.

He searched her face for a sign, and found it. Her eyes...they gleamed in the moonlight, shining with need.

"Hayley," he whispered. And then, his nerve endings firing in painful anticipation, he lowered his lips to hers and reclaimed what once was his.

Her lips were hot and sweet, and they parted almost instantly, as they always had, welcoming him into the even hotter darkness of her mouth. He groaned, and took it all. His other hand went around her waist, and pulled her body into his, breast to chest, beating heart to beating heart.

She held back maybe three seconds, and then he felt her yield, and sink into him. Her hands rose and threaded themselves into his hair.

Hayley...

Dear Reader,

On a recent trip to California, my husband and I took a short tour of wine country. Like millions of other tourists, I fell in love.

A life in this serene, rolling landscape could be very special, I thought. Days spent in harmony with nature, coaxing rich purple, red and green clusters of sweet grapes from the earth, surely would be healing, soothing, good for the soul.

The story of Colby Malone and his high school sweetheart, Hayley Watson, is the fourth book dealing with this complex San Francisco family, and the one that I knew would be the most emotionally difficult to write. The tragedy of their young love, and the years of exile and emptiness that followed, would leave deep scars. It would take a lot of healing to bring them back to joy.

That's when I knew that this reunion tale should take place against the peaceful backdrop of California's Sonoma Valley. A vineyard that has fallen into ruin, and a pair of hearts almost as lost...both restored by the power of love.

I have loved getting your emails and letters about the Malone brothers! Please let me know how you enjoy this one. Stop by the website at KOBrienOnline.com or email me at KOBrien@aol.com.

Warmly,

Kathleen O'Brien

The Vineyard of Hopes and Dreams

Kathleen O'Brien

™
Harlequin®

TORONTO NEW YORK LONDON
AMSTERDAM PARIS SYDNEY HAMBURG
STOCKHOLM ATHENS TOKYO MILAN MADRID
PRAGUE WARSAW BUDAPEST AUCKLAND

Recycling programs
for this product may
not exist in your area.

ISBN-13: 978-0-373-71766-8

THE VINEYARD OF HOPES AND DREAMS

Copyright © 2012 by Kathleen O'Brien

Printed in U.S.A.

ABOUT THE AUTHOR

Kathleen O'Brien was a feature writer and TV critic before marrying a fellow journalist. Motherhood, which followed soon after, was so marvelous she turned to writing novels, which could be done at home. A Floridian, whose soul thrives on the flatlands and sunshine of her native state, she believes there will always be a special place in our hearts for the sights, smells and sounds of the place where we were born.

Books by Kathleen O'Brien

HARLEQUIN SUPERROMANCE

1015—WINTER BABY*
1047—BABES IN ARMS*
1086—THE REDEMPTION OF MATTHEW QUINN*
1146—THE ONE SAFE PLACE*
1176—THE HOMECOMING BABY
1231—THE SAINT†
1249—THE SINNER†
1266—THE STRANGER†
1382—CHRISTMAS IN HAWTHORN BAY
1411—EVERYTHING BUT THE BABY
1441—TEXAS BABY
1572—TEXAS WEDDING
1590—FOR THE LOVE OF FAMILY
1632—TEXAS TROUBLE
1668—THAT CHRISTMAS FEELING
    "We Need a Little Christmas"
1737—FOR THEIR BABY
1746—THE COST OF SILENCE

*Four Seasons in Firefly Glen
†The Heroes of Heyday

HARLEQUIN SINGLE TITLE

MYSTERIES OF LOST ANGEL INN
    "The Edge of Memory"

Other titles by this author available in ebook format.

CHAPTER ONE

FOR THE MALONE family, party meant pizza.

Because the family business was a string of pizza restaurants, the three Malone brothers had more or less started eating it in the cradle. For as long as Colby could remember, the family had celebrated every occasion—holiday, birthday, anniversary, whatever—with platter after platter of Diamante's signature hand-tossed Margherita pizza. Their kids loved it, their friends loved it. Even their girlfriends loved it, or at least pretended to. Otherwise, they became ex-girlfriends in a hurry.

The only time anyone refused Diamante pizza was when one of the Malone wives was pregnant. It was half joke, half legend in the family—for the Malones, morning sickness took the form of an extreme aversion to pizza.

But today, at his brother Redmond's engagement party, Colby couldn't eat a bite. That was a first. Also a first: the chattering of the family and the chaos of the children irritated him.

After the toasts were raised—California zinfandel for the grown-ups, and lemonade for the kids who had graduated from milk—Colby found himself standing slightly apart from everyone, in the shade of an old leather oak, watching the black shadows of clouds try to smother the silver fire of sun on the bay.

Every few minutes, he'd check his phone to be sure the party noise hadn't drowned out the sound of its ringing. Finally, he put it on vibrate, then shoved the thing back into his pants pocket and cursed silently. That old bastard wasn't going to call, was he? This was simply another of Ben Watson's eternal manipulations.

After a few minutes, Colby saw Red lean down and whisper something to Allison. Then Red peeled himself away from her, something he rarely did, and ambled over to Colby.

Colby almost laughed at the casual air Red adopted. He'd used it himself a million times, to escape sticky situations, or to disguise his real intentions. At the moment, Red was obviously trying to hide the fact that he was worried about Colby.

"I'm fine," Colby announced as Red drew closer. His voice sounded a shade too tight, so he added a smile. "What part of *kid overload* don't you understand?"

Red laughed. "I hear you. Good thing the weather cooperated today. Where else could we have taken this thundering horde?"

It had been Nana Lina's idea to make the party an afternoon picnic, at her Belvedere Cove house of course, where the grounds swept down to the bay and everyone had plenty of room to run and scream and play. The family had expanded like wildfire over the past few years. Kids everywhere now, and not one of them had a single quiet, obedient gene in his DNA.

Matt and Belle's pair, Sarah and Sam, were miniature tornadoes, and had just about ensured the family was banned from any restaurant the Malones didn't own. Red's new fiancée, Allison York, had a little boy who didn't walk yet, but crawled as if he had a jet pack in his diaper.

And of course David Gerard, who had become like a brother, had two kids. Colin, just turned three, never stopped talking and acted like a Malone even without the blood tie.

Ten minutes ago, Red had been trying to teach Colin how to burp the alphabet. Good thing David's wife, Kitty, was busy tending their newborn, Tucker, and hadn't noticed.

Colby was the only male in the family without an offspring. The only one who didn't attend family functions accompanied by a U-Haul full of strollers, bouncers, pedal-operated zoom cars and dolls with glittering zombie eyes and high robotic voices.

Red leaned against the tree, the picture of innocence. After a moment of silence, as if the thought had just occurred to him, he spoke. "So. Did Watson call?"

"No." Colby resisted the urge to look at his phone again. "They might not have let him out of the hospital today after all. That might have been wishful thinking. You know how he is."

They all knew how Ben Watson was. An overweight drunk, who was closer to hitting seventy than anyone had ever expected him to be. A bad-tempered fiend who lived alone and didn't do anything but watch his sweet little Sonoma Valley vineyard go to rack and ruin around him.

Well, over the past few months, he'd done at least one other thing. He'd pestered Colby, trying to sell him information about Ben's daughter, Hayley, who had disappeared with her mother and sister seventeen years ago.

"He'll call," Red said softly. "If not today, then to-morrow."

Damn it. Colby didn't want pity. Not even Red's. He was already regretting opening up about the whole mess. He'd coped perfectly well, alone, with Ben Watson's first few calls. He'd even made an appointment to see the old guy—six appointments, in fact, over the past three months. Ben kept cancelling for one trumped-up reason after another.

Colby had finally called his bluff and told the old bastard to go to hell. But then, a week ago, Ben had phoned one last time, like a desperate poker player raising the stakes, going all in. He'd said he not only knew how to find Hayley, but he also had information about the people who had adopted Hayley's baby.

That had come out of the blue, like a sucker punch. As soon as Colby could breathe again, he knew he had to talk to someone. Nana Lina was the obvious choice. She was the only one who had known there ever was a baby in the first place. But Nana Lina wasn't strong these days. A year or two ago, she'd been diagnosed with atrial fibrillation, A-fib, a heart condition that they were trying to control with medication.

But she still had mystery spells, days when she didn't get into Diamante at all. They hadn't yet been able to persuade her to consult another doctor. She said her regular internist Dr. Douglas was fine. It was nothing but the slowing down of age. Maybe she was right. She was almost eighty now.

Still, he wasn't going to upset her with what might just be another false alarm.

And so he'd told Matt and Red instead, enduring their quiet shock as best he could. They'd both advised him to go see Watson, to get the information at any cost, and decide later what, if anything, to do with it.

Then Ben Watson had a heart attack, and he'd been in the hospital ever since. He refused to talk to Colby over the phone, refused to say anything until he was released.

Which was supposed to happen today. But even though it was nearly six o'clock, the phone still lay like a useless stone in Colby's pocket.

"Why the hell can't he just write a letter?" Red sounded irritable, defensive for his brother, as of course he would be. They'd been each other's safety nets since they were orphaned as teenagers.

Shrugging, Colby tugged a leaf off the oak. Its brown center spread out in blotches of red and yellow, ending in green tips that he tore off with sharp twists, as if they were a surrogate for Ben Watson's throat.

The smoky odor the leaf released smelled like every October of Colby's life. This month, that smell, had always reminded him of Hayley. And if it still reminded him of her now, after seventeen Octobers spent with countless other women, he had a feeling it always would.

Red was still ranting. "Watson always was a control freak. Frankly, I don't know how his wife stood it as long as she did."

Colby made a noncommittal sound. He didn't like to think about the years Mrs. Watson had endured in that mission-style vineyard house. Colby should have called the police. He should have guessed that those bruises Hayley always attributed to tussles with her younger sister must have been something more sinister. But he'd been a privileged eighteen-year-old from a loving family. He'd never seen domestic violence.

He'd been so lucky, though he hadn't realized it at the time.

"I was just wondering…" Red glanced over at Colby. "I wonder if Ben even knows anything, really. I wonder if he's stringing you along, enjoying getting your hopes up. And, even if he does, who says it really concerns you? I mean…at the time, you didn't think the ba—"

"Allison is looking for you, Red," Colby interjected before his brother could finish that sentence. He wasn't going to consider the possibility that Ben Watson was lying. That the old man didn't know where the child was.

That Hayley's unborn child might not even have been Colby's baby.

After carrying guilt around all these years, surely he wasn't going to get this close to an answer, only to have it ripped out from under him, like some stupid cartoon character standing on a nonexistent ledge.

This week, waiting for Ben Watson's call, had been difficult. He wanted to believe Ben had real information to sell. He had to believe it. He looked out at his family, spreading across the sloping green lawn, laughing, dancing, eating pizza… They all looked so damn contented. Even little Colin, who had eaten a slice too many and was holding his stomach and crying, was one lucky kid surrounded by love.

So many happy endings. And endings that hadn't been easy to find. Once upon a time, David's romance had seemed impossible, and Matt's road had been pretty bumpy, too. And Red—well, that relationship was nothing short of a miracle.

So the idea that Colby might be able to atone for his one supreme sin, the idea that he might be able to salvage something from the wreckage his younger, arrogant, teenage self had created...

Was that so much to ask?

His hand went toward his pocket one more time. Just as his fingertips touched the metal, he felt it vibrate. As he pulled the phone out, he glanced up at Red, who frowned, obviously aware this might be the moment.

Colby answered it, angling his side to Red, away from the party, needing at least a fraction of privacy. He listened for a minute, then hung up with cold fingers.

Red leaned in closer, his voice tense. "What, damn it? Was it Ben?"

"No," he said. He turned back to his brother, careful to keep his face expressionless. It wasn't difficult, oddly, because everything in him seemed to have turned to stone. "No. It was Ben Watson's vineyard manager. Ben is dead."

IF THIS HAD BEEN A MOVIE shoot, Hayley Watson thought wryly, it would have been the perfect morning to film a funeral scene. Overcast, with silvery threads of far-off lightning in the swollen western sky. Theatrically dreary and bleak.

In the cold October breeze, a willow tree swooned

against a nearby oak, whispering its grief. A wet, gray fog floated a few inches above the grass, swirling, dipping curious tendrils into the six-foot hole in the ground.

The hole where Hayley's father's casket would be lowered, as soon as this naive-but-well-intentioned minister stopped trying to put a cheerful spin on the brutal old devil's life.

Hayley tried to listen, but the eulogy was pure fiction, and she felt as if she, too, were floating a few inches above it all. The mournful willow and the fingering fog reminded her of a ghost story her mother had read them one Halloween, long, long ago. The picture in the book had looked just like this cemetery. She and her little sister, Genevieve, had quivered with excitement, wiggling under the bedcovers, wondering what the ghost would do.

Then her father had burst into the house, red-faced and pop-eyed with wine. "Lazy bitch!" He'd grabbed the book and grabbed her mother's arm. "I'll give you something to be afraid of!"

Hayley shivered, as if she were ten again. As if her father were alive, instead of lying in that casket, the one he'd picked out in his elaborate prepaid package, bought a dozen years ago, indicating he'd finally started to realize he wasn't immortal.

She tried to form a picture of how he must look inside it—burly arms folded, eyes closed, face molded into serenity by the mortician.

But she couldn't see him. It had been too long. All she could remember was color, and sound and fear.

And then somehow, as if she'd gone into a fugue and

missed the wrap-up, the service was over. The boyish minister had picked up her hand, but she couldn't feel her fingers sandwiched between his two consoling palms.

"Ms. Watson. Hayley. I'm sorry I didn't know your father better, but—"

Don't be.

The words were on the tip of her tongue. But why say them? Why say anything except the most basic conversational conventions? She wasn't here to make friends or right wrongs. She wouldn't be attending this man's church or seeking his counsel. She was here to sell the neglected vineyard, if anyone was dumb enough to buy it, pocket the money and go home.

Home to Florida, where she had a life, and new dreams. The best dream of all was waiting for her there.

"It's all right, Pastor Donny." He'd asked her to call him that. He must not realize how silly it sounded. "You did a wonderful job. It was lovely."

He beamed. "Thank you. I'm sorry, too, that the day was so…" He waved at the restless trees, as if they were an added insult. "And the fog—if we'd held the service later in the morning…"

"It probably won't lift before noon," she said.

The sudden certainty shocked her. She hadn't set foot in Sonoma County for seventeen years. She'd made a home an entire country away, in the flatlands of Florida. So why did she remember this fog so clearly? Why did she remember its tickling intimacy against her ankles? Why did she know, in her bones, that it wouldn't disperse for hours?

"I guess not." Pastor Donny shook his head. "Well,

I should let you talk to your friends. I'm glad so many people came. It's good that you're not alone today."

She heard his unspoken disapproval of whoever had let her make this trip alone. She wondered who he thought she should have brought. Her mother died several years ago. Just two weeks ago, she'd broken off her relationship with Greg Valmont, the only serious boyfriend she'd had since leaving Sonoma. Genevieve had recently been promoted at her CPA firm, and was working eighty-hour weeks.

After that, there was no one else to ask. The kind of life the Watson women had lived since they ran away didn't exactly encourage intimate friendships. Her coworkers at the dress shop where she did the books would have been shocked to hear she even had family back in California.

She followed the pastor's gaze toward the cluster of people who stood awkwardly by, clearly waiting to offer her their final condolences. She'd greeted them briefly at the funeral home, but the number had swelled since then. God knew who all had arrived while she was lost in thought.

When she'd decided to attend the funeral—and not just let the prepaid package carry on, like a bad play, without her—she'd known she'd have to cope with this.

So she put a smile on her face, just the appropriate amount of lip curve, and turned toward them. She'd practiced this expression in the mirror of the airplane bathroom a mere three hours ago. She wanted to convey gratitude, and a sense of the solemnity due at the burial of any human being.

Even Ben Watson.

But she had no intention of pretending grief. Her pride wouldn't allow it. And besides, a few of these people undoubtedly already knew her story and were here purely for the lip-smacking entertainment of seeing how she handled herself.

She caught a glimpse of a small, thin man moving toward her. Roland Eliot—definitely not one of the gawkers. He had worked for her father since she was a little girl. When she'd arrived at the funeral home this morning, a full half hour late, she'd been shocked to see him here, waiting patiently with the others. She thought surely he'd retired or come to his senses years ago.

"Miss Hayley," Roland said, his voice somber and his round gray eyes shining. "It is a joy to my heart to see you again. I thought I would never—"

"Roland," she responded with her first real emotion of the day. The week. The decade? She reached out and hugged him. He smelled the same as ever, soap and earth. "It's wonderful to see you, too."

"This is my granddaughter, Elena." With nudging palms, he ushered forth a preschooler who had black curls and his round gray eyes. She couldn't be more than four. "Elena, this is Miss Hayley, the girl who sleeps in the treetops."

The little girl's eyes grew even wider. She nodded gravely, but she didn't speak.

Hayley wasn't sure she could speak, either. She had forgotten that Roland used to call her that. Suddenly she felt the wind in her hair, and the rough oak bark of her favorite perch against her cheek. She could almost see the blues and greens and browns of Foggy Valley Vineyard spreading out below her, the hills dipping and swelling and the rain on the green leaves sparkling under the summer sun.

She shook herself free of the trance. Old memories, even this one, were like ghosts. They would float in front of your eyes, and bring sights and smells and pains. But in the end, they were not real. Phantoms, with no more power than this fog.

"Would you come by the house and visit us later, Miss Hayley?" Roland's face was more lined now, but as sweet as ever. "Later, when you've had time to rest? We could talk. Miranda has made a casserole."

"Of course," she said. "I'd love to catch up."

Other people were waiting, so she contented herself with that. She pressed his hand and smiled her good-bye. And, touching his callused fingers, she felt a little stronger.

Over the next few minutes, she greeted half a dozen well-wishers. Some were vaguely familiar. Others were people who must have entered her father's life long after she left it. She found her rhythm, and luckily everyone was on his best manners. No one asked overly personal questions. A couple of glances were full of pity, and she caught whiffs of the expected curiosity, but overall nothing she couldn't handle.

Then she heard a voice so familiar it made her heart skip.

"Hayley?"

She looked to the left, and stopped breathing. She'd been doing so well. But now the facade of calm dignity fell from her shoulders like an unzipped, oversize dress.

There he was, the ghost of all ghosts, the man who

had haunted her dreams for at least a decade—and still strolled into a stray one occasionally, even now.

Colby Malone.

A barrage of images assaulted her. Black-haired and blue-eyed. Expensive and dangerous and divine.

Seventeen years older, of course—thirty-five now, though it was hard to believe. But he was somehow shockingly the same. Tall, athletic, still not an inch of fat. Shoulders broader than before, broader than a dream could capture. The faint prettiness he'd possessed in youth had made way for a powerful virility.

"Hello, Hayley," Colby said. His voice was deeper, too, more polished and yet more intense. And his jaw, though freshly shaven, hinted of a sexy stubble he'd have to work hard to repress.

He was, in some ways, a stranger. And yet, even under all this new virility, he was still the boy she'd known. He put out his hand. She twitched, as if she needed to avoid an invisible slap. A weak sensation passed liquidly through her knees—and her first truly coherent thought was, how could she ever have believed that what she felt for Greg Valmont was love?

Somehow, she held herself rigid. She was tougher than this. Naturally, she had considered the possibility of running into Colby Malone while she was here. But she hadn't really believed he'd bother to drive forty minutes to attend the funeral of a man he had despised.

She'd told herself she would be fine, no matter what. She'd loved him, and then she'd hated him, and now she simply didn't give a damn.

"Hello, Colby," she said politely. She gave him exactly the same measured tone, practiced smile and cool hand she planned to give everyone here today. "How nice of you to come."

He shook her hand. It pleased her to note that he seemed more uncomfortable than she was. As he should be.

She let go in precisely the correct number of seconds.

"How are you?" Her tone implied the question was perfunctory and didn't require an answer. She didn't leave time for one. "How is your grandmother? And Red and Matt? I know you must need to get back to San Francisco, but I do hope you'll give them my best."

And then she turned to the next person, who thankfully had begun to push closer, eager to be recognized.

She took a split second to be sure of the identification, then smiled. It was her music teacher, the kindhearted martyr who had listened to her murder scales every Tuesday afternoon for five years. A "frivolous" expenditure her mother had insisted on, like Gen's ballet lessons—no matter how their father had roared.

"Ms. Blythe! I'm so glad to see you. You'll be relieved to know I've given up the piano entirely, for the good of mankind."

Ms. Blythe smiled, as if she might accept the light joke as the truth of Hayley's feelings. But then she shook her head. With tears spilling down her plump cheeks, she wordlessly reached in and scooped Hayley into a hug.

With her chin pressed against Ms. Blythe's fleshy shoulder, Hayley shut her eyes. It was so strange, being welcomed by these old acquaintances, almost as if she'd never left. But seventeen years. Didn't they know seventeen years was too long, and she wasn't the same person at all?

Didn't Colby Malone know that? What could he possibly have hoped to gain by coming here? Didn't he know that, if she'd wanted to see him, she could have called or written or come back to San Francisco anytime? If you wanted to communicate indifference, was there a more convincing method than seventeen years of silence?

Eyes still shut, she counted to three, telling herself that when she opened them, Colby Malone would be gone.

One. He had to know how she felt. The Malone boys had always been smart, all of them. Good judges of people—able to make you feel utter bliss or abject misery, with just a well-chosen word. Colby, especially, as the oldest, was the gang leader. Witty and caustic and clever.

Two. Surely someone that sharp could easily read between the lines and grasp how unwelcome he was here. He had to know.

Three. She opened her eyes.

He was gone.

CHAPTER TWO

COLBY GOT BACK to the house at Belvedere Cove just before dark. On a Wednesday evening, he expected to find his grandmother in the kitchen, whipping up the Diamondberry cheesecake that was her signature dessert at Diamante. The restaurant served it only straight from her kitchen, only Friday and Saturday nights.

They could have sold each piece a hundred times over, but Nana Lina knew better than to cheapen it by glutting the market. This way, every customer who succeeded in getting a slice felt as if he'd won the lottery.

But when Colby arrived, the kitchen was dim and undisturbed. The row of copper-bottomed pots lined up on the wall burned in the fading light that filtered in through the big back window. He glanced into the kitchen garden, but no figure, no shadow moved through the sunset-tinted herbs and grasses.

Surprised and slightly unsettled, he moved to the foyer and took the curving staircase two steps at a time. When he got to his grandmother's door, it stood ajar, but he knocked anyway, softly, in case she was sleeping.

"Come in," she called. "I'm just resting."

When he pushed the door open, he was met by cool, dark shadows, which surprised him. Nana Lina's room—once Grandpa Colm's room, too—was always brightly lit and welcoming. Powdery blue drapes framed a picture window that overlooked the bay, and the view was so dazzling no one ever pulled them shut. Even while she slept, moonlight spilled in, making the silver picture frames and perfume bottles glow, and redoubling itself in the mirror over her vanity.

He'd spent many an hour in this room. Maybe because he was the first grandchild, he and Nana Lina had a special bond, even before his parents died. He'd always brought her his treasures, whether they were rocks with interesting fossils or cloudy shards of sea glass. She had always seemed to understand why a little boy would find these bits of debris fascinating.

"You sleeping?" He tried to sound casual, though he knew it was futile. She had a sixth sense about her family. Even the best lies set off her internal alarm.

"What an absurd question. Since when have you known me to sleep during the day?"

She had a point. She might be nearing eighty, but she would always be the heart and soul of Diamante. She might not always be the first in and the last out every day, as she once was. But she was still a force.

As his eyes adjusted, he realized she wasn't in bed. She was sitting on a comfortable armchair, her feet propped on an upholstered ottoman. She reached up and twisted the knob of her table lamp, which immediately covered her in honey light.

"Don't try to smooth-talk me, Colby Malone." Her brown eyes twinkled at him. "What you *really* want to know is whether I'm sick."

"Mind reader." With a smile, he raised one eyebrow. "Well, are you?"

"I don't know. I might be."

His shoulders braced, and his chest tightened. He'd asked for an answer, and he'd received one. He should have known she wouldn't sugarcoat it.

"What makes you think so?"

Her robe was made of silk, a pattern of elegant blue roses against a silvery background that matched her hair. She leaned forward from the waist and lifted the hem, which had puddled softly on the floor around the ottoman. She settled the fabric more demurely around her ankles, then repeated the motion with the other side.

Even that much activity seemed to leave her slightly breathless. He wondered why he hadn't noticed sooner that her condition had grown this much worse.

He'd observed that she tired easily. That she stayed in bed later, turned in earlier. He'd asked her to get a second opinion about the A-fib, but she'd waved it off. Sometimes she seemed absolutely fine. Just Sunday afternoon, at Red's engagement party, she'd played dolls with Sarah for hours....

But she hadn't played chase or hopscotch, or pushed anyone in the swing—all activities she ordinarily loved. He frowned, wondering how long she'd been compensating for...

For what? God forbid it was something serious. He suddenly realized how impossible it was to imagine a world in which Nana Lina didn't rule with an affectionate iron fist.

"Nana Lina, what's really going on here? I know you've resisted seeing a new doctor, but clearly the meds aren't working. I think it's time to call—"

"I'm a little short of breath, that's all," she said, folding her hands in her lap and giving him her most regal look, which commanded him to remain calm. "Occasionally I get dizzy, and I don't always have the stamina I should. Perhaps you boys and your ever-expanding offspring have finally worn me out."

He chuckled. "It's not us. You could handle us and the Holy Roman Army, too. With one hand." He moved to her side, not the least bit intimidated by her scolding tone. "Look. I don't like this. Like it or not, you're going to see Dr.—"

"Dr. Douglas?" She tapped his arm. "Don't you start adopting a bossy tone with me, young man. I am perfectly capable of recognizing when it's time to consult a doctor. I have an appointment with him next Tuesday morning, in fact." She squared her shoulders. "Sidney will drive me, so don't get any ideas about coming along to babysit."

Colby subsided, relieved. As long as she had the appointment, he could relax for now. He'd talk to Matt and Red. One of them would find a way to tag along and get some answers.

"Yes, ma'am," he said in a phony meek voice. He sat on the edge of the bed, glancing at the magazine she'd been reading. It was a catalog of elaborate play sets designed to look like castles, forts and other magical places. One touted itself as Atlantis.

"You know," he said, "if you don't want the ever-expanding offspring to sap your life force, maybe you shouldn't keep adding to the Disneyland you've built in the backyard."

She whisked the magazine away with a low tutting sound. "I was just relaxing my mind after studying last month's receipts, and Red's proposal for the new store in Sonoma." She fiddled a little more with her robe. "He seemed to think you might be heading over there today to take a look at it. Did you?"

He chuckled again. She was good, but they all knew each other too well. "Don't try to smooth-talk me," he said in a teasing imitation of her words. "What you *really* want to know is whether I went to Ben Watson's funeral."

She smiled, well aware the jig was up. "Well?" She tried to mimic his one-eyebrow query. But no one could beat Colby on that look, not even Red and Matt, though they'd spent their youths trying.

She settled for a scowl. "Well? Did you?"

He nodded. "Yes. And the answer to your next question is yes, as well."

She lifted her chin haughtily. "My next question?"

"Yes. You want to know whether Hayley was there. It's a fair question. I know you've wondered…all these years… We've all wondered. So yes, she was there. And she looked fine."

"Fine?" His grandmother rolled her magazine into a tube, the paper making a soft, slithering noise. When it was safely rolled, she gripped it firmly. "What does *fine* mean?"

As Colby searched for the right words, a vision of Hayley Watson rose before his mind's eye. What did *fine* mean? What exactly should he say to describe how she'd changed?

The transformation was dramatic. She had changed so much that, on a conscious level, he probably wouldn't have recognized her. He might have had to ask someone to be sure—except that his body had identified her in an instant. The minute he laid eyes on her, every nerve ending he possessed zapped him with a small electric charge.

"She looks completely different. Poised, and well dressed. And she was wearing her hair—" He put his hands up and waved them around his head, trying to imply the complicated halo-braid kind of thing that had controlled her long, thick, honey-colored waves. "I don't know. Sophisticated. She looks like someone else, actually."

His grandmother tilted her head. "That's the best you can do? I never saw her—or her hair—back then, except in pictures. Why would I care how she wears it now? I mean, does she look well? I don't expect happy, given the circumstances, but does she look healthy and content?"

Did she? "Healthy, definitely. Content... I really couldn't say. Maybe."

Nana Lina nodded, tapping the magazine roll against her knee slowly. "Well, considering that until today we thought she might be buried out in that vineyard, along with her mother and her sister, I guess that's saying a lot."

Colby cut his gaze to the picture window, even though the drapes were shut and there was nothing to see.

Nana Lina didn't know, of course, that twelve years ago, Colby had hired a private investigator to make sure all three Watson women were safe and well.

All he'd wanted, really, was to know that Hayley was alive. He shouldn't have to spend the rest of his life wondering if there might be any truth to the local rumors that three ghostly beauties went weeping through the Foggy Valley Vineyard on nights with a full moon.

Finding them had cost a lot of money—at least, it had seemed like a lot to a twenty-three-year-old still in his last year of law school. Obviously the women had been desperate to keep their location a secret, in case Ben decided to follow them and make good on his threat that, if Evelyn Watson didn't live with him, she wouldn't live at all.

Something Colby's investigator did must have tipped Evelyn off, because when Colby got the information and tried to contact her a few weeks later, all three of them—Evelyn, Hayley and Genevieve—were gone. No notice at their little apartment or their jobs. No forwarding address.

He hadn't tried again. He knew Hayley didn't want to see him—not if she'd remained away, without so much as an email, for years. And if she didn't want to see him, he wasn't going to push himself back into her life.

Especially since the investigator had told him there was no sign of a child. Colby had tried to forget it— forget her. She'd probably been mistaken about the baby, done some wishful thinking and turned a late period into an imaginary pregnancy. He'd been just a few months shy of going to college, and she had been desperate at the thought of being left behind. It wouldn't, he told himself, be the first time a clingy female had tried to will a baby into being, just to trap a man.

It made Colby cringe to remember the bullshit he'd try to sell himself.

"Did she seem surprised to see you?"

He looked up, and he saw Nana Lina's gaze on him, sharp and probing.

"She didn't show it, but of course she must have been. She kept it short and…" *Sweet* wasn't really the right word, was it? "We exchanged only a very few words, and they weren't particularly personal." He ran his hand through his hair. "Let's just say she doesn't wear her heart on her sleeve anymore."

"Good." His grandmother nodded, and he wondered what that tone was in her voice. It didn't sound judgmental. It sounded…sad. Was it possible that she, like Colby, had found herself regretting what they did all those years ago? If she regretted what they'd said, what they'd done, she'd never showed it.

"Was she alone?"

Alone? For a minute, he could see Hayley standing there, in the wooded cemetery, with a storm building around her, and her dead father's casket hovering just above the big rectangular hole. He wasn't sure he'd ever seen anyone who looked *more* alone.

"Her mother wasn't with her," he said, deciding he'd just stick to the facts. "Neither was Genevieve."

"No husband? No boyfriend?"

He shook his head. "No. No husband. No wedding ring. No—" He took a deep breath. "No family at all. At least, no one who had come to the cemetery with her."

And he left it at that. But he knew that, as they sat

there in silence, they were both thinking the same tangled thoughts.

No husband, no boyfriend.

And no sixteen-year-old total stranger, no nameless child with black hair and blue eyes who might, just might, have been Nana Lina's unacknowledged great-grandson.

"THAT'S BEAUTIFUL, ELENA," Hayley said, picking up the crayon drawing Roland's granddaughter had made for her as they played and colored after dinner. "Is that me?"

Elena nodded somberly, and Hayley was glad she had interpreted it correctly. At four, the child's art skills were still fairly primitive, but it seemed to be an illustration of a girl sleeping on the fragile tip-top branches of a tree. The stick figure, which stretched out rigidly across the branch, had bright yellow hair, and the tree's leaves were made of circles so vigorously drawn they had left little green crayon shavings behind on the paper.

The four of them—Hayley, Elena, Roland and his wife, Miranda—had gathered in the front room of the little square adobe foreman's house—well, what used to be the foreman's house, back before her father started selling off the acreage. Now it was just Roland's house.

Hayley smiled over at the serene-faced man, who sat in his straight-backed chair near the fireplace, watching quietly. "You must have made this tree story seem very romantic."

"He made it seem a great deal *too* romantic," Miranda said, with the rote sound of someone who had gone over this subject many times already. She had been gathering toys, and briskly tossed a bunny into a wicker basket. "When in fact climbing tall trees is quite dangerous, and if anyone I know ever tries it, she'll be punished!"

Hayley glanced at Elena, whose eyes had grown large. "Your meemaw is right," she said. "I wasn't being smart. If I had fallen, I would have been hurt very badly."

But could anyone have stopped her? She'd been about six when she fell in love with climbing the vineyard's encircling trees. Maybe it was because, up high, she felt entirely disconnected from the misery inside her house. She imagined herself a fairy, with an acorn cap for a hat, bluebells for shoes and wings made of rainbows and wind. She was small enough to hide in the leafy branches, and sometimes she wouldn't come down, even when she knew her mother was calling.

One day, when she was seven, her parents had a bigger fight than ever before, and she'd climbed higher than ever before. Fifteen feet up in the black oak tree, she fell asleep. According to Roland, the household was utter chaos as they looked for her—her mother frantic, her father furious, bellowing her name.

Roland was the one who had found her, sound asleep, luckily wedged between the huge trunk and the thick branch, her legs and arms dangling like pale pink tinsel. Though he had been nearly fifty, arthritic and tired from a long day in the vineyard, he'd climbed up and brought her down to safety.

The fight, she'd learned later, had been ignited by the news that her mother was unexpectedly pregnant again.

After Genevieve was born, Hayley never climbed another tree. She still longed to escape, but one glimpse of the baby, and she knew she had to keep her feet on the ground, in case Genny needed her help.

She looked at Elena now, wondering if this little girl would also feel the need to find a private place, to pretend her life was different. Miranda had whispered earlier, as Hayley helped her prepare dinner, that Elena's mother had run off a year ago, and probably wasn't coming back.

It was hard for Hayley to comprehend that. She knew, of course, that not everyone wanted to be a mother. But this beautiful, fragile little girl...

It was so easy to damage a child like this. And so hard to make her whole again.

Her heart fluttered softly, as she thought *if I had a child*...

No. Not *if. When.* When she had a child, she would wrap him in so much love he could never break. She had a sudden image of the blue-striped wallpaper of the nursery she'd begun at home. And the five bright bluebirds that circled on the mobile above the crib. Only three more months now.

Three months, and the cradle that had been empty for so long would be filled.

She considered telling Roland and Miranda. They would be happy for her, even if they didn't know the whole story, even if they could never understand how much this new baby would mean.

Her heartbeat sped up at the thought. Still, she wasn't ready to share the news yet. She felt guarded, superstitious...haunted by the memory of the last time she'd had news like this to share. As if something terrible might happen if she spoke of it too soon.

They were all silent for a few minutes, listening to the crackle of the fire and the muted piano notes of Chopin on the sound system. Her heartbeat settled down—the magic of the Eliots working on her as it always had.

Hayley had spent many hours just like this when she was a child—back then, Genevieve would have been the toddler scribbling at the coffee table. By the time she was ten, Hayley had hoisted her fat, laughing baby sister onto her hip, and started coming here to the refuge of this little house, with the foreman who understood her better than her own father.

She'd given Genevieve as many hours of peace as she could. But she always had to go home again, eventually.

Just as she did tonight.

The only difference was that, tonight, her father would not be there. She wouldn't have to wonder, as she entered the house, whether this was a good night or a bad one. Whether he was drunk or sober. Whether, when her mother turned around from the kitchen sink, she would be crying, or bleeding.

Banishing the image, Hayley stretched, shaking off the sleepiness caused by the plane ride, the time difference and the emotional day. The funeral had been harder than she'd expected. And seeing Colby...

No. She wouldn't think about Colby. She put her hand softly on Elena's dark curls, then stood up from the cushy leather sofa.

"I guess I should head back to the big house," she

said, trying not to sound ten years old again, and scared. "Miranda, the casserole was fantastic. Thank you so much for—"

She swallowed, suddenly unable to find the words to thank them for everything they'd done, not only tonight, but all those years ago.

"I'm sorry I couldn't call," she said in an abrupt switch of topic. "Or write. But Mom was always terrified. Always covering our tracks. She said any contact with our old lives would be fatal. She was so sure Dad would find us."

Miranda came over and hugged her. "We knew," she said. "Your mother wrote us once, just so that we wouldn't fear for you. She didn't tell us where you were going, merely that you had to leave. We understood, maybe better than anyone, why it was necessary. We knew your father."

"Did he start looking for us right away? He never tried to contact us, but obviously his lawyer knew where we were." For a long time, she'd wondered whether all the subterfuge, the fake names and the prepaid cell phones and the cash-only living, had been required. Somehow she couldn't imagine her father staying sober long enough to launch a serious tracking campaign. Her mother had feared he would hire someone to find them, but Hayley had her doubts about that, too. She'd never known her father to turn loose of an extra penny for anyone but himself.

"I don't think he looked for the first several years. Not until his first heart attack, I'd guess." Roland rose, lifted Elena into his arms and came to stand near his wife, who still had her arm around Hayley's waist.

"I got the feeling he was afraid that, if your mother came back, she might press charges against him. She wouldn't have, for herself, but for *you*..."

His gaze was gentle, but worried. She wondered how much he knew about that night, the night they disappeared. Someday, maybe, she'd tell him, but not tonight. She was so tired, and she still had to face that house.

Would it be better, she wondered, knowing that her father was in a casket, six feet underground, never to come storming through the doorway again? Or would that make it worse?

"Why don't you stay here tonight?" As if she'd read her mind, Miranda squeezed her waist. "I can put some sheets on the sofa."

When Hayley started to protest, Miranda laughed. "Really, it's quite comfortable. Ask Roland. He's out here half the time. We call it the doghouse."

Elena giggled, then buried her face in Roland's shirt self-consciously. Hayley couldn't remember ever meeting a shyer child. But Elena's laughter was adorable, and even its echo filled the room with a sense of light and optimism.

Hayley thanked Miranda, but firmly insisted that she wanted to stay at the big house. Roland offered to walk her back, but she turned that down, too. He'd already done everything he could to make the place welcoming. They'd put her bags there earlier, before dinner, and Roland had shown her around the downstairs, just as if she'd never seen the place before. That brief tour had been enough to let her know that he'd cleaned up a little bit, and added a few homey touches, as if he'd guessed she might plan to stay there, at least for a while.

A vase of blue hydrangeas on the kitchen table, a casserole and a big glass pitcher of fresh milk in the refrigerator. Even a book or two on the end table.

The Eliots' sensitive presence permeated the place—or at least it had this afternoon. It had been light outside, then, the storm passed and sunshine streaming in through the windows. A playful wind had teased the fluffy, October-brown heads of the grapevines.

But she'd lingered so long, coloring with Elena, that it was full night now. She shot a glance out the front window, where the silhouettes of trees moved darkly against the silvery sky, and thought of the still, empty rooms waiting for her.

She shook the feeling away. Dark or light, it was just a house. She would be fine.

The Eliots stood on the front porch and watched her walk up through the vineyard. She turned at the last minute, before the dip in the land would obscure the view, and waved merrily. She was fine. They waved back, and she thought she heard Elena call her name.

She waved again. *She was fine.*

Then she turned back toward the large, two-story adobe house, with its orange-tile roof and arched colonnades extending to either side like outstretched arms. Roland must have put some lights on timers, because several of the windows glowed, long rectangles of amber illumination that should have looked welcoming, but instead just looked unnatural, knowing, as she did, that no one was inside.

Weeds grew up at the edge of the rows of vines, making the path uneven. She kept her eyes on the ground and kept going, glad for a reason to ignore the strange tricks the moonlight played with the wire supports. In her peripheral vision, the metal winked randomly, giving the illusion that something moved among the leaves.

Ridiculous. *She was fine.* No matter how haunted the place might feel, she didn't believe in ghosts. And even if she had believed, she wouldn't give her father's ghost the satisfaction of driving her out of the house again. He was gone. He had not found her, or Genevieve. Even her mother had died in peace. They had all officially survived him.

So that meant she was the one with the power now. She would sell his house, and his vines, and go back to Florida. She would never, ever think of him again. He would rot here, unloved and unmourned.

Hey, Dad, she thought, gathering her courage into one bitter burst of defiance as she neared the house. *I'll give you something to be afraid of.*

But just as she put her foot on the first step of the porch stairs, a large, man-shaped form disengaged from the arches of the western colonnade. She froze in place, her hand foolishly at her throat.

Oddly, her first thought was—could it be Greg?

But that was silly. Why would Greg follow her here, all the way from Florida? He was a doctor. He was busy. People depended on him. Even though his behavior during their break-up had given her a mild case of the creeps, he wasn't a fool. He wouldn't chase after a woman who had already made it painfully clear that they were through.

"I'm sorry to come so late," the man said politely. He continued to move forward, his steps silent on the tiled floor, until he emerged from the shadows. Moonbeams silvered one side of his face.

The light only confirmed what she already knew, from those few syllables of his husky voice. The man who waited here in the darkness wasn't a ghost, and he wasn't Greg.

Once again, she had come face-to-face with Colby Malone.

CHAPTER THREE

"I'M SORRY," he repeated carefully, trying to give her time to adjust. "I didn't mean to frighten you."

"I wasn't frightened," she said.

But he knew that was a lie. Her face was white. She would naturally be twitchy, coming back here after so long, especially under these circumstances. And no woman alone in an isolated spot could possibly enjoy seeing a stranger emerge from the shadows.

Weird, thinking of himself as a "stranger." But no other word applied anymore. Back when they were teenagers, he'd waited for her so many times, right in this very spot. Once, her face would have lit up to see him, and she would have leaped into his arms, their two bodies stumbling back into the shadows with urgent kisses but no words, so that no one inside the house would hear.

Now, she froze at the sound of his voice, as guarded as a doe confronted by the barrel of a rifle.

"What do you want?"

Okay. He hadn't expected a warm welcome, and apparently he wasn't going to get one.

"I know it's late, and you must be tired. I was going to wait until tomorrow, to give you time to settle in. But—"

Her face remained impassive. "What do you *want?*"

"Just to talk. I hoped we could talk."

"Wouldn't the phone have been better?"

He tilted his head, appraising this pale, collected woman who bore only the most superficial resemblance to the girl he used to know. She still had on the gray flared skirt and short jacket she'd worn to the funeral, but it didn't look rumpled even after all these hours. The Hayley he used to know was always dressed in bright colors, always dashing about, her pink cheeks looking slightly fevered, her golden hair flyaway and fabulous.

"I would have been glad to call," he said reasonably. "Except, I don't know your number, remember? If you left Sonoma tomorrow morning, I wouldn't have any idea how to find you again. I don't even know what name you answer to these days."

That wasn't an exaggeration. He knew what name her mother had been using when his investigator found her, a dozen or so years ago. But she'd moved again after that, and the second time he tried to find her, about six months ago, no one of that name existed.

Bottom line was, he didn't know anything, not one single solitary thing, about her anymore. He hadn't even been a hundred percent sure she was staying here at the vineyard house, until he'd seen the car with rental plates in the front drive.

Leaving the cemetery after her brush-off today hadn't been easy. The gossip among the other locals attending the service had been that Hayley would be staying in town, at least long enough to settle up her father's affairs. But who knew if that was really true?

Who knew whether Hayley Watson might decide to disappear into the night all over again?

"Colby," she began, then stopped. She folded her arms, tucking her hands under them, as if the night air had chilled her fingers. "I don't want to be rude, but I really don't think we have anything to talk about, do we? As you said, it's been a very long time. We are both different people now, and the past— Well, it just isn't very relevant anymore."

He heard the dismissal in her voice. His pride bucked once, trying to throw him, trying to compel him to walk away. The past was dead to her? *Irrelevant?* Okay, fine. She meant nothing to him, either.

He choked off the inner voice. That was just the huffy and stupidly proud teenager inside him talking. He was disappointed to discover that, after all these years, remnants of that self-centered jackass still remained.

"Hayley," he said, working hard to avoid sounding pushy or entitled. "I understand that you may well have nothing to say to me. But I have something I'd like to say to you."

She wasn't going for it. He could tell by the way her full lips tightened. "Colby, I—"

"Please," he said. It wasn't a word she—or anyone else—had often heard him utter. "I've owed you an apology for seventeen years, and I don't want to lose this chance to make it now."

She clearly hadn't been expecting that. Her arms fell to her sides, as if suddenly limp with surprise. Her gaze scanned his face—though he had no idea what she searched for.

Finally she nodded. "All right," she said. "I'm listening."

He glanced at her lightweight suit—a sign that wherever she lived probably didn't have the chilly nights of Northern California. "You look cold. May I come in?"

"No."

He had to laugh at little at that. "You aren't planning to make this easy for me, are you?"

She smiled, too, but it was cool and unamused. "I'm not planning to make it difficult for you, if that's what you're implying. But neither do I see why it's my responsibility to make it *easy*. I didn't ask for an apology. I don't require one, and I don't think you owe me one. As I said, I believe it's all ancient history, and best left alone. You're the one who seems to feel it's important."

He felt slightly stunned, as if her attitude were an unexpected jab to the gut. He had really been a romantic idiot, hadn't he? All this time he'd secretly thought that, if they were ever to meet again, even if it was by accident, on a crowded street, some irresistible force that had survived the whole heartbreaking mess would draw them together.

Like some sad sack in a chick flick, he had actually believed that, if he ever got the chance, he could make things right.

He looked straight into her blue eyes. "God, Hayley. Are you really as indifferent as you sound?"

"Yes." She shrugged. "I've had seventeen years to make peace with what happened. I'm not saying I wasn't angry at first. I'm not saying it wasn't hard. But it's over. Life goes on."

She didn't so much as blink. He couldn't detect even

a microscopic flinch that might have suggested she lied. She still looked only tired, cold and slightly irritated.

"Fair enough," he said, refusing to be thrown off his course, even by that total apathy. "But the truth is, I'm still looking for the peace you say you've found. I've done a lot of soul searching over these years. And I think the reason I can't get over…over what happened… is that I was to blame."

She didn't contradict him. She just waited.

"What I did was indefensible, Hayley, and I've never had a chance to apologize. I've never had a chance to make it right."

He thought he might have seen a sudden flare of color in her cheeks, but when she moved, the light changed and the pink disappeared. She shook her head once, crisply. "Those are children's words, Colby. There's no making it *right*. In the real world, there are some mistakes you can't undo."

"Maybe. But I still need to say it. I need to tell you how sorry I am. From the minute you told me you were pregnant, I knew the baby was mine. I knew there hadn't been any other men—boys…"

He cringed at the awkward phrasing. Where had all his fantasy speeches gone? In his dreams, he was so eloquent he moved her to forgiving tears. Where had all those powerful words gone now that he finally needed them?

She still didn't move a muscle. But she was clearly listening. And that was something, he supposed.

"I was a coward. Partly, I was afraid of what my grandparents would think."

Hayley's news had come only three months after

his parents' deaths. He'd been eighteen, grieving, both for his beloved mom and dad, and for the loss of his sheltered, idyllic life. His grandparents, who were the strongest people he knew—then or now—had been devastated by the death of their son and daughter-in-law, but they'd rallied for the sake of the boys.

How could he tell them he'd let them down already? How could he add another disaster to their burden? That's actually how he had thought of the baby: *a disaster.* And so he'd jumped through the one escape hatch he could find. He and Hayley had always been off-again, on-again. For a teenager, the forty minutes between San Francisco, where Colby lived, and Sonoma, where Hayley lived, might as well have been half a world away.

He'd met her the summer he was sixteen, when he'd been sent to the little Sonoma town of Ridley to work in the Diamante just opened there. They'd dated all summer, and they'd hung out sometimes over the school breaks, too—Christmas, Thanksgiving, Halloween, spring break. Then the next two summers, he'd requested the Ridley assignment again, and picked up right where he left off with Hayley.

But that last summer, they'd broken up. A fight about Colby going away to college. The gossip that had been circulating among their friends was that she'd taken up with her old boyfriend, who was consoling her in the time-honored way.

Colby's pride had been wounded when he heard the rumors, and he wasn't in the mood to believe her when she came to him, crying and saying she was going to have a baby. He told himself she was just trying to trap him. She'd been needy all summer, fearful that he'd forget her when he left for college in the fall.

So that's what he had told his grandparents—that, even if her story was true, and she was pregnant, Hayley had probably slept with another boy. She was just trying to pin it on Colby because he was richer and a better catch.

Whether they believed him or not, they backed him. They'd met with Ben and Evelyn Watson and told them that their grandson felt he was being wrongly accused. They requested a paternity test.

Nana Lina and Grandpa Colm had seemed satisfied, and reported that the meeting had been more civilized than they'd expected, given Ben Watson's temper. But that night, without a word to anyone—including Colby—Evelyn Watson and her two daughters had driven off into the night, never to return to Foggy Valley Vineyard.

He'd been shocked, but selfishly, a little relieved. Colby had told himself, and his grandparents, that her flight was proof enough that she'd been lying.

It made him wince to think of all that now. Who did that kind of thing? He'd been one mixed up young man that year, but that was no excuse.

Hayley seemed to have been digesting his statement about being afraid to tell Nana Lina and Grandpa Colm. Her jaw and mouth had a hard, cynical set—and he suddenly realized he had seen that look before. That was the look she had turned on him when he asked her if she was sure the baby was his.

"Your grandparents worshipped the three of you," she said. "Their perfect young lions. They might have been angry, but they would never have stopped loving you. They would have supported you, no matter what."

She was right, of course. His fear of letting them down had been only part of his motivation for being such a fool. The other part was even less admirable.

"I know," he admitted grimly. "The truth was, I simply didn't want to believe the baby was mine. I was spoiled, and I was excited about going away to college—the girls, the parties, the whole frat-boy experience. I didn't want to be tied down with a wife and baby."

"No," she said, her tone dry. "Of course you didn't."

He didn't blame her for the sarcasm. It was a lot less than he deserved. In fact, he might have felt better if she had yelled at him, or slapped him or burst into tears. The idea that he was too unworthy to hate made him feel cold, and strangely empty inside.

"At first," he went on, "when I heard you were gone, I was actually relieved. I know how it sounds, but it's the ugly truth. I thought I'd dodged a bullet."

"Charming way to put it," she said evenly. "But tell me. When, exactly, did you have this epiphany? When did you change your mind about the bullet? Seventeen years ago?" She smiled. *"Yesterday?"*

"It happened gradually," he said, trying to be as honest as possible. But there was no easy answer. At first, he'd been in deep denial, joining a fraternity and partying like a madman, collecting great-looking coeds the way little boys collected baseball cards. He hadn't let his grades slip, either. Straight A's all the way, right through Stanford Law. It was as if he had to do everything, have everything, be everything—to justify not being the father of Hayley's baby.

"I think it really started when I got out of law school. Before that, I kept so busy, and I was focused on that grand prize, the big law career. When I got a job at my first-choice firm, I expected to be completely happy. But I wasn't. I started trying to figure out why."

She made a dismissive sound. "The quarter-life crisis. Everybody has one. I think it's rather classic, when you first start spending all day behind a desk, to wax sentimental about the carefree days of youth."

"That's fair," he said, determined not to argue. "I'm sure there was some of that."

He'd thought exactly the same thing, at first. Quarter-life crisis. The "is that all there is?" moment. He'd started playing handball on his lunch break, sailing the *MacGregor,* the family sailboat, every weekend, and finding even more beautiful women to date. He'd cut back on sleep, so that there could still be plenty of time for fun.

He got exhausted. But he didn't get happy.

"Anyhow, that was when it started." He wondered if he should tell her about the private investigator, but immediately decided against it. This was an uphill battle already. "But it was more than that. Finally, I just stopped kidding myself. I had been a selfish bastard, and I was going to have to pay for it the rest of my life. I was never going to forget about the baby you were carrying when you left that night. I was always going to be haunted by the knowledge that, somewhere, someone was raising a child who should have been ours."

For the first time, she looked confused. "Someone? What do you mean 'someone'?"

"The…people, the family…" he said, stumbling in the face of her transparent bewilderment. What did that mean? Was she shocked that he knew? "The people who adopted the baby."

She drew her head back. "What makes you think I gave the baby up for adoption?"

"Because—your father said…" He couldn't seem to form words correctly. "Your father said you did."

"Ah." She smiled coldly. "My vicious, drunken father? And you believed him?"

"Yes."

"I see," she said. "Did this piece of information by any chance come with a price tag?"

He shook his head. "He told me that much for free. If I wanted to know how to find the adoptive family, though, he said that was going to cost me five thousand dollars. But I never got the information, and he never got the money. He died before I got the chance."

"Well, that's a bit of good luck. Because you would have paid all that money for nothing. He might have given you a name, maybe even an address. But it would have been bogus. You should have known that. Like so many alcoholics, the man was a consummate liar."

He frowned. "How can you be so sure it would have been bogus? Are you saying you didn't give the baby up for adoption?"

His mind was reeling. When his investigator found Hayley, he had reported that she was single, living with her mother and sister and no one else. Eventually, when Colby finally stopped kidding himself that the pregnancy had been fictional, he'd assumed she'd decided on adoption. It had made a cruel sense. Alone, on the run, three women supporting themselves with menial jobs that required little documentation… How could Hayley have done right by a child in that scenario?

Besides, in his heart of hearts, he couldn't believe that she would have raised their child, year after year, milestone after milestone, birthdays, and Christmases and acne and math, without ever sending Colby so much as a photo. Her heart couldn't have been that hard, no matter how reprehensible his actions had been.

"Hayley, answer me. Is that what you're saying? You didn't give the baby up?"

"No," she said flatly. "I didn't give the baby up."

He couldn't take it in. "But—then—where is he?"

"He's nowhere," she said dully. "There is no baby."

"I don't believe it." He shook his head stubbornly, not caring how stupid it sounded. "I don't believe it. You weren't lying to me that night."

"No. I wasn't lying. When I left here seventeen years ago, I was pregnant, and you were the father. But you've tortured yourself all these years for nothing. There is no baby."

He took in a breath, trying to fill his lungs, though no matter how hard he tried, they continued to burn from lack of air.

"Why?" His mind suddenly latched on to an unthinkable answer. "Oh, my God, Hayley, surely you didn't—"

"Damn it. No." Her eyes narrowed. "Look, I don't talk about that night, Colby. Not ever, not to anyone. But—because—well, let's just say for *old times' sake,*

I'm going to tell you this. Though, as far as I'm concerned, you have no right to know. There is no baby, because that night—"

Her eyes sparkled where the moonlight touched them, though her face was still as hard as if she were a mannequin, made of plastic. "That night, before we even reached the California state line, I lost him."

He was still shaking his head. He felt as if she spoke in some language he had never heard before. "*Lost* him?"

"Yes," she said. "In the backseat of my mother's car, surrounded by our suitcases and everything we could get out of the house without waking my father, I miscarried."

She put out her hand. For a confused second, he thought she might be reaching for him, and he started to extend his own. But then he saw a key glint. She placed it neatly, deftly, in the lock and turned it. The front door opened with the squeak he'd last heard seventeen years ago.

"Go home, Colby," she said, her tones frighteningly detached, though he suddenly saw that her face ran with tears. "There is no child, and there's nothing more for us to say."

CHAPTER FOUR

HAYLEY WAS TREMBLING when she shut the door behind her. She pressed her back against the wood, flattening her shoulder blades, as if she thought Colby might try to batter it down. Her breath came quickly, like a heroine in a horror movie who had escaped just in the nick of time.

She scoffed at herself for being so melodramatic, hoping she could force herself to calm down. But as she surveyed the room in which she'd taken refuge, she didn't feel much better.

The foyer was dimly lit by a fake chandelier. Its dangling pieces of plastic, which had been cut to look like crystals, were furred with dust.

The entry area had seemed sad, pale and oddly smaller when she and Roland had dropped by this afternoon. It looked much different now that it was night, now that she was alone.

And it teemed with memories. She glanced toward the far end of the hall, where it led to the kitchen, half expecting to see her father stalking through the opening, a beer in his hand and fury in his face.

For several long seconds, she stood there, heart racing, caught between two unbearable memories. Colby hadn't left the porch, she knew that from the utter silence behind her. But inside… She shut her eyes, as if that would keep her father's ghost from materializing.

Oh, God, she shouldn't have come back to Sonoma. She shouldn't have set foot in the vineyard, in the graveyard or in this house. So what if her father had wanted to be buried here, on Sonoma soil? She hadn't needed to come. She should have hired someone to clean the house, as Genevieve had encouraged her to do, and then hired a real-estate agent to sell the property.

But, no—she'd called that plan too cowardly. She'd been so sure she could handle returning home. It would be healthy, she'd told Genevieve. She'd been so confident that, after seventeen years, she'd grown up enough to put her old life into its proper perspective.

She shook her head, feeling her hair pulling free of its careful French braid as it snagged on the tiny splinters of the old door. This was her lifelong sin—the sin of idiot optimism and dogged pride. From the time she was a little girl, she had always believed she could do anything. Sleep safely in treetops, marry the handsome superstar, flout the alcoholic tyrant.

She could still remember the last night she'd ever entered this house and thought of it as home. She'd come in late from work—one of the other cashiers had called in sick. For once, she hadn't even been thinking about her dad, and whether he would be drunk. She'd been locked in her own private hell, worried about the baby, and angry about Colby's inexplicable reaction to the news.

But not yet terrified. She had no idea that the Malones had come here to see her parents. She'd believed that her secret was still safe. And, fool that she was, she believed that, once Colby got over his shock, he would come around. He'd do the right thing. He loved her. Sure, they'd fought, and they'd broken up, but everyone knew that was just temporary. They belonged together. He loved her.

The minute she shut the door and dropped her keys on the hall table, her father appeared out of nowhere.

"You disgusting slut," was all he'd said, and then she felt something hard and cold crash against her head. Later, she learned it had been his full beer bottle. She didn't even remember falling to the floor, and she didn't remember the rest, either, thank God. Had he kicked her as she lay there? Or had he hauled her up by the hair and punched her? The next day she'd found her own hair all over her shirt, so maybe he had.

She only knew that, sometime much later, her mother had helped her into the living room—just to the right of this foyer—and onto the sofa. Her consciousness went in and out with a fiery, strobelike effect.

She didn't ask why her mother wasn't taking her upstairs and putting her into bed. She assumed that she wasn't able to climb—one of her hips hurt so much she thought it must be broken. But hours later, when her mother woke her again and helped her limp in total silence out to the car, she realized that her mother had kept her downstairs because that would make the escape easier.

She knew, somehow, that she mustn't cry out, though she had figured out by then that it was her leg, not her hip, that really was broken. As she exited the house, the moon was full on the vines. Genevieve already sat in the front seat, clutching her ballerina bear, her face like a white button at the window.

Her mother had brought pillows and blankets, and made a sort of bed in the backseat for Hayley. She lay gingerly down, hugging herself against the pain, and passed out again.

She woke somewhere near the Nevada line, screaming. Someone was stabbing her stomach with knives, and blood streamed out of her, soaking the denim of her jeans.

"No," she had cried, squeezing her legs together in spite of the pain. "No…no…no…"

The sudden sound of a car engine snarling to life returned her to the present. She sagged against the door, relieved. Finally, Colby was leaving.

Somehow, just knowing she wouldn't have to face him anymore tonight brought back a little of her courage. She moved away from the door, deciding it was time to do something practical.

She pulled out her cell phone and put a call in to Genevieve. To her surprise, her sister picked up on the first ring.

"I was just about to call you!" Genevieve's musical tones sounded scratchy, as if she'd worked too many hours today. "I've been on since about six this morning, but they finally gave me a couple of hours to sleep. How are you? Did you make it through the funeral okay?"

"I'm fine." And, as always, the sound of her little sister's voice was enough to bring the world back into balance. "The funeral was uneventful."

"Did you decide to stay at the house after all? I still think a hotel might be—"

"No hotels, silly. There's a lot to do before we can put the place on the market, and I might as well get started." Hayley had to smile at herself. Two minutes ago, she'd been seeing specters and barring the door against demons of the past, but now she was back to sounding like the bossy big sister.

"Honestly, I'm fine. The place isn't as big a mess as I'd expected, actually."

Genevieve sounded unconvinced. "Well, that's good, but…"

"But nothing." With her sister's voice as company, Hayley marched resolutely up the stairs. "I want to hit the ground running in the morning. So I'll just turn in early and—"

She stopped at the door to her old room. Confused, she swiveled on the landing, checking the layout to see if she'd become disoriented. But no, this was her room.

Had been her room, anyway. In Hayley's mind, the room had never changed. It had remained exactly as she left it that final afternoon, when she dashed off, late to work as usual.

She could remember every detail. She'd bought a new pair of sneakers, because she got a discount now that she worked at the sports superstore. She'd stuffed the empty box into the trash can, but she hadn't quite been able to make it fit, which she knew would make her father mad. The shirt she'd worn to school—white with a scoop neck trimmed with blue sequins, all the rage that year—had been tossed onto the foot of the bed, abandoned for her uniform shirt.

And, of course, all along the edge of the mirror were pictures of Colby. Laughing, confident Colby, with his arm around her, about to dunk her into the pond, or leaning over her, dangling a cluster of grapes just above her open mouth.

But none of that remained. Instead, a sea of boxes greeted her. Such a mess. She couldn't have stepped two feet inside this pink-walled room if her life had depended on it.

It had become the rubbish closet. Maybe, she thought, that was where all the possessions they'd left behind had ended up. Maybe, somewhere in there, was her diary, which her father had undoubtedly found when he took the mattress off her bed. And the pregnancy test, which she'd wrapped in a bag and stuffed behind her winter sweaters.

"What's wrong?" Genevieve sounded concerned. Hayley wondered how long she'd been silent.

"Nothing," she said. She launched into a light-hearted description of the sweet touches Roland and Miranda had added to make the house homier.

As she talked, she closed the door on her room and tried Genevieve's. Though he'd left the pink ballerina border along the ceiling, her father had turned Gen's room into some kind of home gym. A treadmill, a weight bench, a stationary bike.

She tried to picture him using any of this—and she suddenly realized that her mental picture was seventeen years out of date. She'd asked for a closed casket, and she hadn't felt the slightest urge to look inside.

She shut the door. She kept talking, but her mind was sending out a string of painful questions.

Had he changed very much as he'd grown older? He would have been nearly seventy. He'd always been a little overweight. Beer belly, mostly. The lawyer who phoned had said her dad died of a heart attack. Was it a surprise? Had he been warned about his habits? Had he spent the last months of his life in the converted exercise room, trying to sweat out a lifetime of booze?

"Hayley," Genevieve said, breaking into her mindless chatter, obviously not buying it for a minute. "You sound funny. What's going on?"

Hayley had just opened her father's bedroom door. Finally, a bed, the same dark walnut four-poster her parents had always shared. The same picture window that overlooked the vineyards, though the drapes were closed now, and the overhead light fixture was missing a couple of bulbs.

Now she understood Miranda's furrowed brow, her anxious eyes, when Hayley insisted on coming up here to sleep.

She knew within ten seconds that she couldn't. Without her mother's presence, her mother's perfume to lighten the air, the whole room smelled like her father.

The odor was sickly sweet, with a hint of sweat and leather. Heavy undertones of beer, though someone, probably Roland, had emptied all the trash cans and even wiped down the nightstand.

She would never forget that smell. Her uniform shirt, covered in the beer from her father's broken bottle, and the sweat of her own pain as she lay on the sofa, had smelled exactly like this room.

But if this was the only available bed...

Her only other choice would be the divan in her mother's sewing room, if it were even still there. But that was where her mother had always retired, so that she could be alone to weep.

She could use the sofa downstairs. That might have a certain poetic justice. Her last night here, and her first night back, spent on its leather cushions…

"Nothing's going on," she said to Genevieve. "I'm just realizing the place is messier than I thought. I think…" She hated to admit defeat, but, damn it, she wouldn't sleep a wink here tonight. "I think you may be right about the hotel."

"Of course I am," Genevieve said, clearly relieved. She laughed. "Get the heck out of there right now. I know you believe you're invincible and everything. But you're only human, Hayley. Like the rest of us."

Hayley shut her father's door quietly, and headed down the stairs. She wasn't defeated. She was just tired. It had been a long day. The funeral, then Colby…

Tomorrow, she thought. Tomorrow, she'd return to being invincible. Tonight, she just needed to sleep.

SHE ARRIVED BACK AT THE vineyard just after dawn the next day—or so her watch said. It was difficult to tell if the sun had risen, because a heavy gray rain pummeled her windshield as she made her way up the hill. It pounded the dirt rows between the vines, too, exposing stones and cigarette butts—plus all manner of debris unidentifiable in this dim light. A small but telling sign of how her father had neglected this property, maybe for a long, long time.

Up ahead, the main house squatted, dark-eyed and unwelcoming, under the low-hanging clouds. The car bounced over the driveway ruts slowly, and she finally came to a stop inches from the front porch.

For a minute, as she debated whether to bother with an umbrella, she exchanged scowls with the two-story structure. Wet and muddy definitely wasn't its best look.

But sleep had restored her determination, and she was ready. A cup of take-out coffee nestled warmly against her thigh, and a banana from the hotel's free breakfast poked out of the zipper of her purse. She'd scraped her hair back in a ponytail so tight her ears stuck out like a leprechaun's—not exactly flattering, but functional.

In the backseat, she had a blank book for jotting notes, a plastic crate to collect important papers and a box of a hundred and forty-four garbage sacks in which to dump the rest. Plus, her cell was newly loaded with phone numbers—lawyers, real-estate agents, estate-sale agents, charitable organizations hungry for donations, carpenters, glaziers and house cleaners.

To heck with the umbrella. It wasn't as if she'd put on makeup, or fixed her hair. This was work. Dirty work. Suddenly eager to get going, she flung open the car door and darted out into the rain.

Two hours later, the rain hadn't let up. The big kitchen windows looked like they were covered in watery gray curtains, but she had all the lights blazing. She was on her knees in front of the pantry, a yawning garbage bag on the floor next to her, when the doorbell rang.

"It's open," she called out, hoping she could be heard over the drumming of the rain. She figured it had to be either Roland or Miranda, who both had promised to stop by and help if they could.

The shiny black plastic bag rippled as a gust of damp, earthy wind swept through the shotgun arrangement of front door, hallway and kitchen.

"Back here," she said, reaching for a clear container of what looked like pasta dipped in pepper. When one of the grains of pepper began to move, she realized her mistake. She dumped it, container and all, into the bag and turned as Miranda arrived in the doorway.

"I'm sorry we didn't get to that," the older woman said, shaking raindrops from her long, black hair as she folded up a glistening umbrella. Her brow wrinkled. "We thought the fridge was more important. Your father wouldn't let us in the house for weeks before he passed, and these last few days, with Roland finishing up the harvest and—"

"Don't be silly. You guys have done so much already. I'll have this cleared out in no time!" Hayley climbed to her feet and embraced Miranda, who smelled like cinnamon, as if she'd been baking. "I'd offer you something to drink, but nothing in here looks safe, except maybe the beer. I've already finished the milk you left."

"I'm fine." Miranda looked around, obviously registering the magnitude of the job Hayley was facing. "I can't stay long, unfortunately. Just until Elena's preschool lets out."

Hayley assured her that was great. And it was—she knew the Eliots meant well, but some of the work she'd have to do here would undoubtedly stir emotions. The kitchen was merely grimy and annoying, but chores like sorting through her old things, or her father's finances…

She'd rather tackle those alone.

Clearly not intending to waste a minute of what time she had, Miranda pulled out one of the padded bar stools that faced the granite island and moved it closer to the counter above the sink. She opened the cupboard door and sniffed.

"Most of these canned goods are probably still okay," she said. "Shall we start a bag for the Food Bank?"

"That one over by the stove is set aside for donations. There's not much salvageable in here, though." Hayley surveyed the still-teeming pantry shelves. She was already on her third garbage bag, and only about half done. "Everything is years past the sell-by date. I guess he didn't cook much. I must have found a dozen empty pizza boxes stacked up in the mudroom."

Miranda laughed. "Yes, we saw the delivery boy head up here maybe four or five times a week. But never Diamante. He still refused to do business with them, even though they're the most convenient. They probably have five locations within ten miles of here."

Hayley paused, her fingers gingerly holding a can that had one bulging side, as if something on the interior was trying to get out. "Really? They've expanded that much? Before I left, they had only the one take-out place in Sonoma."

"They're everywhere. But your father…" She chuckled. "He said their pizza was crap."

Hayley didn't answer. She couldn't. When Miranda said those words, Hayley could almost hear her father speaking. "Arrogant bastards," he used to say when anyone mentioned Diamante. "Think they're better than everyone, but under those expensive suits, they're still just hash-slingers. And it's crappy hash, too."

He lied, of course—everyone knew Diamante had the best pizza. Strictly a California product, though. The first few years after she left Sonoma, Hayley had suffered intense cravings for the honey-sweet crust and signature red sauce.

"I guess he never forgave the Malones for…for Colby," Miranda said tentatively. "I mean…Colby and you."

Hayley tightened her jaw, but managed a smile and a shrug. "That was just the most recent sin. The truth was, Dad never forgave the Malones for deciding not to carry Foggy Valley wine in their restaurant anymore."

Miranda nodded. "They were the first, weren't they? But not the last."

That was an understatement. Diamante had merely been the leading edge of a tidal wave of vendors abandoning the tiny winery Ben Watson had been neglecting for years. The Foggy Valley label had been well respected when Hayley's mother's parents were alive, but by the time Hayley was thirteen, the winery end of the business was only a memory. A few bits of silver equipment quietly rusting away in an abandoned barn on the eastern edge of the property.

Miranda probably regretted opening old wounds, because she changed the subject smoothly and began asking Hayley questions about her life in Florida. Hayley was happy to tell her all about Genevieve, and her promotion, and the little string of dress shops where Hayley had worked for the past fifteen years.

She still kept the baby news to herself.

They talked until nearly noon, by which time great, lumpy garbage bags covered fifty percent of the blue-tiled kitchen floor. All the cabinets were empty, except for the ones that held plates and mugs, glasses and other housewares. The estate-sale agent would be selling things like that. And soon.

Thankfully Hayley had learned that she wouldn't have to maneuver through a complicated probate process. When her father's lawyer had telephoned her with the news of the death, he explained that Ben had set up a trust that made the transfer of assets quite simple. He'd left everything to Hayley and Genevieve, no mention of his wife, as if he'd known quite well that Evelyn Watson had died long ago.

Hayley hadn't been sure which shocked her more—that her father obviously knew where to tell his lawyer to find her, or that he'd been sensible and proactive enough to organize his will into a trust.

For some reason, both bits of information made her chest tighten, as if there might have been a great many things she didn't know about her dad.

But the important thing was, if she worked hard, and luck was with her, she could be free of all this much sooner than she could have imagined. She could hardly wait to see what the real-estate agent said the property was worth. She hadn't cared much about money for the past seventeen years, but with a baby coming into her life…it would be wonderful to have a cushion in the bank.

At fifteen minutes to twelve, Miranda's cell phone beeped. She knotted off her last trash bag and whisked her hands together briskly. "Gotta go. School's out at noon, and Elena cries if I'm even a minute late."

Hayley nodded. They had spent some of their time this morning discussing Elena's fragile situation, so no more explanation was needed. After a full year, the little girl hardly remembered her mother—consciously, at least. But she had a dread of abandonment that proved how deep the damage went.

When Miranda left, Hayley decided to take a break. She needed to stretch. She needed to smell something other than stale beer bottles and stagnant garbage. She grabbed the banana from her purse and wandered into the living room, where she could sit on the sofa, the most comfortable piece of furniture in the house, and watch the rain on the vines while she ate.

She wasn't aware of falling asleep. She wouldn't have thought, in fact, that she even could sleep on this sofa, however comfortable, because of the memories it held. But suddenly she was waking up to the sound of the front door opening. Her heart raced in her chest as she awkwardly hoisted her sluggish body to a sitting position. The banana peel tumbled to the carpet at her feet.

"Miranda?"

But that didn't make sense. Miranda was picking up Elena...wasn't she? Hayley looked at her watch, but it wasn't there. She'd taken it off while she was grubbing around in her father's trash. She rubbed her eyes and started to move toward the hall, but before she could take a step, a man appeared in the doorway.

Colby...?

But no. The contours were similar to Colby's, but the colors were all wrong. It looked like…

What was wrong with her? Her mind really wasn't working. Maybe she was still dreaming. Because the man in the doorway was…

It couldn't be. He was in Florida, three thousand miles away.

"Greg?"

The tall, broad-shouldered man smiled. His thick blond hair glistened with raindrops, but its robust waves, which had earned him the nickname "Dr. Delicious" among the nurses, were unconquered.

"Sweetheart," he said in his most mellifluous voice. He came closer. "I couldn't wait for you to come home. I missed you too much. So I came to you."

He held out his arms, and in spite of how gorgeous he was, a ripple of distaste ran through her. This wasn't right. It was incredible, literally impossible to believe, that he could be here. And…somehow creepy. Why on earth had he come all this way, across the country, on what could only be a fool's errand?

The last time she saw him, she had told him it was over, and she'd meant it. She had been clear-cut, almost insultingly explicit. No two ways about it. She meant it, and he *knew* she meant it.

"What on earth are you doing here, Greg?"

He took another step closer, bringing him near enough that she could smell his aftershave. Lime sharp enough to sting her nostrils. Instinctively, she folded her arms across her chest. Her heart still beat too fast.

And then her head cleared.

"Wait." She narrowed her eyes. "How did you even know where to find me?"

He must have seen that she was very angry, but, as always, he remained calm, so calm. Greg Valmont, M.D., had the perfect bedside manner, the manner that had guided dozens of pregnant women through labor.

Always under control. Never ruffled or impatient, like her father. Never a hint of wildness, arrogance or danger, like Colby.

For Hayley, that soothing manner had always been one of his most appealing characteristics. Finally, she'd thought, here was a man who wouldn't ever hurt her.

Until that day two weeks ago. The day he lost his temper.

"How," she repeated, "did you know where to find me?"

"I'm so sorry, Hayley," he said with a disarming candor. "I know I shouldn't have, but I was going crazy, wondering when you'd be back. I looked at your mail. I saw the letter from the lawyer."

"What?"

He tilted his head, and even in the watery light, his green eyes were brilliant, flecked with golden lights. "I know it was wrong, but you left it open on the hall table."

"You went into my house?" She was almost breathless with fury. "How? You gave me back the key."

He shrugged, looking sheepish. "I had another copy. I'd forgotten about it completely, until… Look, sweetheart, I know you're upset. But you should have told me about your dad. You shouldn't have faced this alone. I could have been here for the funeral."

"I didn't *want* you here for the funeral. I don't want you here now. We aren't together anymore, Greg. You do remember that we broke up two weeks ago?"

The corners of his mouth moved into little-boy-sad position. "I remember that we had a fight. I remember that I goofed up, badly. I upset you. But surely one little mistake isn't enough to destroy a relationship as beautiful as—"

"It wasn't a little mistake," she said, not wanting to hear the rest of that sentence. Once, that kind of talk might have sounded romantic. But now she heard how false it was, how manipulative. It made her skin crawl. "It was a huge mistake. A fatal mistake. And if it hadn't been enough to destroy our relationship, this would have done it anyhow."

"This?"

She waved her hand toward the door. "Yes, this. This—*invasion* of my privacy. You broke into my house, and now—"

"Hayley, that's not fair. I may have been foolish, but I didn't break into anything. I had a—"

"And now you've stalked me clear across the country. You've violated my privacy here, too. You have no right to be in this house, or even in this state. I want you to give back that key, and then I want you to get out of here. Immediately."

Apparently without thinking, he reached out his hand. He got close enough for her to feel the heat of his fingers, but she whipped her arm aside before he could touch her skin.

She felt her cheeks start to burn, as her heart pumped

oxygen faster than her veins could absorb it. Her throat tightened. "Don't. You. Dare."

For a split second, she was embarrassed, as if she were making too big a deal out of what was obviously a friendly touch. But then she caught it—the sudden tightening around his eyes, the momentary hardening in their green depths. It was the same look she'd seen that night two weeks ago, when she'd told him she didn't feel like making love.

He was furious. Not just angry, not just upset. Furious.

That night, he'd been aroused, and he hadn't been able to cover his frustration. He'd grabbed her irritably, and he'd kept kissing her, pressing her toward the bed as though she were a moody, difficult female who was just confused about her own needs.

He probably believed that, once coaxed into starting, she'd end up enjoying herself. He hadn't realized that she was the last woman in the world he should handle in such a way. Since that night seventeen years ago, she hadn't let anyone touch her in anger. *No one.* She had zero tolerance—no amnesty for "one drink too many," or for "just joking around" or for abject apologies and roses.

"I'm sorry you feel that way, Hayley," he said, shifting his shoulders wearily, as if he were a long-suffering martyr accepting an unjust verdict. "I thought you might have come to your senses. I hoped you would realize that any...extreme emotions I have are just because I love you."

"Get out," she repeated. Chills rippled through her veins, every instinct recoiling from the weirdness of the whole situation. It was bad enough that he'd done all these things—break into her house, go through her mail, stalk her to California—but to act as if it was all forgivable, because he "loved" her…

Good grief! How crazy was he? And how had she missed the signs during the whole year they dated? Had she been hypnotized by his good looks? Lulled by the fact that he was a doctor, and everyone she knew adored him?

"If I go now, Hayley, I won't be back," he said, but still gently, as if he merely thought she ought to know.

"I sincerely hope not." Her voice was cold.

Still, he gazed at her with that hurt-puppy-dog look. What if he wouldn't leave? She glanced at the wet world outside, and tried to calculate her chances of getting through the door before he could stop her. Not good. She pulled her phone out of her pocket.

"Get out," she said one last time, her numb fingers poised to hit 9-1-1.

And then, thank God, he did.

CHAPTER FIVE

"YOU SHOULD HAVE seen her face when Douglas said she still had an atrial flutter." Colby had already folded his hand, so while his brothers and David Gerard sweated over the cards, he was free to think back on the comical expression his grandmother had turned on her poor doctor yesterday.

"'Flutter?'" He mimicked Nana Lina's cold outrage. "'*Flutter?* I have never *fluttered* a day in my life, young man.'"

Red, Matt and David all chuckled, clearly sympathetic with the doc. The white-haired internist was at least sixty years old, but Nana Lina remembered him in diapers, so he was always at a disadvantage.

The mood at tonight's poker party was relaxed. Atrial flutter, or fibrillation, or whatever it turned out to be, wasn't great, of course, but it was the same diagnosis Nana Lina had lived with for a couple of years. They'd all been afraid something new had gone wrong.

Colby had guilt-tripped Sidney, his grandmother's chauffeur, into telling him the exact time of Nana Lina's appointment, and he'd shown up at the medical office unapologetically, insisting on being part of the discussion after her exam. The brothers didn't often pre-empt Nana Lina's autonomy, but they'd agreed that this time felt different. Her recent pallor and lack of energy alarmed them, and they'd wanted to know exactly what was going on. She'd protected them most of their lives, and they wouldn't put it past her to hide any distressing news from them now.

"Still…even though she may hate the word, a flutter is a lot like the A-fib we've always known about, right?" Red tossed a couple of chips into the pot, though Colby was sure his brother couldn't be holding much better than a pair of jacks. Red always played recklessly, just as Colby always played conservatively. Matt, the middle brother, played like a middle brother, quietly and without stress. David, another lawyer, had started out pretty rigid, but Kitty's influence on him had been dramatic, and these days he sometimes went for the big, crazy bluff.

"Seems that way." Colby finished off his beer, the last of the night, since he'd be driving. "Douglas says the flutter does carry a stroke risk, though, just like the A-fib would. He thinks if he switches the meds, she'll be fine, but he'll know more when they get the test results back."

They played in silence for a few minutes. No one needed to say what they all knew: a world without Nana Lina was unthinkable. Even David had come to love the old lady as if he were blood-related, partly because she'd embraced the unconventional Kitty without blinking an eye. David loved anyone who loved his wife.

The four men—with the occasional addition of another friend, most often their surfing buddy Stony Jones—played poker every Thursday night, rotating houses so that none of the wives ever actually came to the end of her rope. Tonight they were at David Gerard's cavernous old Victorian for the second week in a row, because Kitty had taken the boys to visit her mother back East.

Colby's phone rang, which earned him scowls from the other men. Cells were supposed to be turned off. Back when they were all single, girlfriends had texted and phoned so compulsively on poker night that no one could concentrate. So they'd put the cell phones away. If there was an emergency, family knew to call the landline.

"Sorry. Forgot." Colby pulled the phone out of his pocket so that he could turn it off. He sneaked a look at the caller ID, and in spite of himself, he scowled. Marguerite. She was two girlfriends ago. They'd been hot and heavy for a couple of months, but when the sweat dried they'd realized they had absolutely zero interests in common.

Well, zero *other* interests.

The breakup had been friendly. He had heard that she'd started something torrid with some low-level pencil pusher at her daddy's stores, which made sense, because she'd definitely had father issues.

Well, good for her—and for the pencil pusher. All's well that ends well, right?

Colby had never expected to hear from her again. And yet this was the third time she'd called today. Some primitive, self-preservation instinct deep inside him didn't like that.

"What?" Matt shot him a knowing glance. "Or should I say *who?*"

Colby held down the power button until the screen

display disappeared. "Nothing important. Remember Marguerite?"

"Oh, crap," Red broke in, slamming his palm against his forehead. "I meant to tell you, I ran into her last week. She was asking about you. Asking if you were seeing anyone."

Colby put the phone back in his pocket. "What did you tell her?"

"You know. That you got drafted, you died, you joined a monastery... Something like that." Red frowned at the newest card he'd been dealt. "I know the script."

Everyone laughed, but Colby noticed David staring at him with an odd look. Nothing unkind, of course. David was always empathetic. *Nice* was his hallmark. But this look had something that reminded Colby uncomfortably of pity.

Colby met the glance with one of his own.

David shrugged, knowing he'd been caught, and called on it. He looked at the large pot, then, with a sigh, folded his hand, too. "I was just thinking...don't you ever get tired of it?"

Colby smiled. "Of women?"

"Of so *many* women. Surely, in the millions of females you've dated, there must have been at least one who..." David shook his head. "Don't you ever think about settling down?"

On the other side of the table, Red and Matt exchanged glances, then studied their cards as if they were about to take a test on them. The brothers all liked David. More than that, they trusted him. They'd chosen him to administer the Diamante driver's fund, a charity that had caused them trouble in the past, when they'd turned it over to someone less upright. David was a great guy. He was like family.

But *like* family wasn't the same as *being* family. In the end, he wasn't really a Malone. He wasn't blood.

And he hadn't ever even heard of Hayley.

"Sure, sometimes I think about settling down, getting married, having a couple of kids." Colby kept his tone light. "Then I look at my two brothers here. And I immediately stop thinking about it."

David's expression didn't change for a long moment, stretching out the silence until it nearly got awkward. At the final minute, though, his features relaxed, and he chuckled, letting his gaze sweep over Matt and Red.

"Yeah," he said, "I see your point. They are pretty damn pathetic."

HAYLEY SLEPT IN THE HOTEL again that night. Greg's arrival had spooked her. She hated herself for being a wimp, but she just couldn't sleep at the vineyard house alone.

The next day, though, she awoke to yellow sunshine filtering in through the curtains, and her spirits lifted once again. She had to smile at her dogged optimism, so illogical, given how this trip had gone so far. A funeral, the ghost of an old love and a stalker. What else could go wrong?

But she couldn't help it. She'd always been like this—hopeful in the morning. She wondered whether she'd developed the trait to defend herself—and Gen—against the horrors of home, or whether it was just coded into her DNA. Her mother's parents, everyone said, had been sunny, positive people.

Gen had inherited it, too, although hers was more fragile. "You keep saying tomorrow will be better," Gen had said bitterly one night when she was about eight. Hayley had been reading her to sleep while a battle raged below them. "But it never is."

"We just need to be patient," she'd promised her little sister. "You'll see."

Maybe it was the books. All those fairy tales she read while she was hiding up in the treetops. Somehow, she'd never quite given in to despair. She had always believed that some sparkling happiness lay ahead of her, if only she could hold out long enough.

When she fell in love with Colby, she'd thought her miracle had finally come. If ever magic had seemed to live inside any human being, it was Colby Malone.

Well, that showed how ridiculous her dreams were, if nothing else did.

Just in case, she called Greg's office, and the service told her the doctor was expected back that afternoon. Good. At least she wouldn't have to spend the day looking over her shoulder.

She and Roland were scheduled to meet at the vineyard at eight, so that he could show her around the property. When she pulled in, she glimpsed his golf cart rumbling around the south side of the house. She was delighted to see that Elena rode in the backward-facing seat, her feet swinging, her chin high, clearly ecstatic to be included.

Returning Elena's wordless but energetic wave, Hayley climbed into the cart beside Roland.

"Hi," she said. She glanced up at the cloudless sky. "Got lucky with the weather, huh?"

He nodded, smiling. "We never have more than two days of bad weather in a row here. You must remember that."

Of course she remembered. She'd forgotten a lot of the practical things, like the smart way to train the vines so the fruit would grow in a line, making picking faster and more productive. But she remembered the weather. She remembered the way Colby's hair curled when the fog and rain dampened it. She remembered how brightly his blue eyes sparkled under a sunny sky.

She remembered how, after she told him about the pregnancy, she had peered into the curtain of rain every night, praying she'd see his car driving up the path. Now that Roland mentioned it, she knew he was right. Just two nights of rain then, too. It had felt like a lifetime.

Once more, she shook off the memories. She needed to focus on what Roland was telling her. The real-estate agent would arrive this afternoon, and it was important to be as informed as possible.

"You know he sold the western flat, right?" Roland paused the cart at the edge of the rolling hill that marked the boundary of the pinot vines. "I wish he'd sold the pinot acres instead, but you know how he was."

She did. In her grandparents' day, Foggy Valley had been seventy acres, with sixty acres planted, all zinfandel grapes. But her father had felt that the other vintners looked down on zin, so he took one block and put in pinot noir. Just an experiment, he'd promised her mother. It had never been successful, but he'd been too stubborn to switch back.

Now the vineyard was a mere twenty acres, only ten planted. And half of that was still the pinot.

"Why couldn't he ever make the pinot work?" She was sincerely curious. At the time, she'd just assumed that her father's nasty temper ruined everything he touched, but that didn't make sense. The zin he grew was apparently delicious. "I mean, pinot grows just fine in vineyards all around here."

Roland gazed pensively over the vines. "I don't know. We've got microclimates all over this area. For instance, it's four degrees warmer down on my acres than it is up here. This site likes zinfandel, that's all. He was too stubborn to accept that."

With one last sweeping gaze over the vineyards below them, Roland started up the cart again, and rolled them toward the zinfandel, the vines that grew between his house and hers. He was right about the microclimates, of course—Roland was a true farmer, and he listened to the land.

"If I were going to keep the vineyard," she said impulsively, "I'd switch it all back to the zinfandel."

Roland laughed. "You weren't even old enough to drink when you left," he reminded her. "How did you develop a preference for the zin?"

"I don't know. I heard the winery guys talking to Dad. Something about their excitement—the way they described the zinfandel. All that talk of flowers and cinnamon and blackberries." She laughed. "It sounded so romantic."

He nodded. "It is that."

"And I love the way the zin vines smell." She took a deep breath. "I can't describe it. Just clean and sweet and…good."

Roland nodded. He, too, inhaled deeply, his chest expanding. "It has a nice nose," he said, with a clear satisfaction. He grew zin, too, on the acres he'd bought from her dad. "Always has."

Behind them, Elena breathed in dramatically. "It has a nice nose," she repeated, aiming for her grandfather's gravity. Roland and Hayley exchanged a look and somehow refrained from laughing.

"So…" Roland turned the cart south, toward the back of the property. He drove slowly, obviously aware of Elena bobbing on the back. He cut Hayley a quick glance. "Does that mean you're thinking about it? About keeping the vineyard?"

"God, no." Hayley shuddered. "You know I could never live here again. Too many memories."

Roland lifted one shoulder. "You could make new ones."

She shook her head. "It's been too long. My life is in Florida now. That's where Gen is. You should see her, Roland. She's gorgeous. Brilliant. Happy. She's got a great job, and a great boyfriend, too. A really nice man. Nothing official yet, but I wouldn't be surprised if he's the one."

Roland smiled. "I'm glad she's happy. That's your doing, you know. You protected that little girl from… from everything."

She put her hand on his arm, in wordless gratitude. She hoped that was true. She had certainly tried.

"But that's her life you're describing," Roland said

quietly. "That great life you've built in Florida—it's all hers. Not yours."

Hayley felt her cheeks flush. He was partly right. Given what a creep Greg had turned out to be, and given that she had stayed at the same dress-store job ever since she got out of high school, she really hadn't built much worth staying in Florida for.

Except for the baby. Once again, she considered telling him, but the circumstances were all wrong. The story was complicated, and Elena was listening. Who knew how much the child might understand—how much might confuse and trouble her?

So she didn't answer, and he didn't push. They rumbled along in companionable silence for a few minutes, passing in and out of the shadows of the elderberries and wax myrtles that rimmed this part of the property. They came to a stop in front of the old winery building, which had definitely seen better days.

They all three got off the cart and wandered closer to the building. Roland plucked a strip of peeling brown paint and tossed it into a rubbish bin nearby.

Roland led the way, holding Elena's hand to be sure she didn't step in any of the tiny tidal pools the rain had left in the patchy grass.

Hayley wondered at all the junk that littered the ground—rusty old cans, disintegrating fruit crates, beer bottles and fast-food paper cups. Maybe neighborhood teens still used the remote spot for trysts. She and Colby certainly always had. The huge old trees provided plenty of shade, and easy cover if someone happened along.

"Wow," she said, whistling. "He really let this go,

didn't he? Doesn't he host the Haunted Vineyard anymore?"

"Hasn't done that for years. I took it over back when I bought the acres, about ten years ago," he said. "We set it up in my barn now, mostly."

She picked her way across the debris carefully, and waited while Roland unlocked the double doors and swung them open.

At first, she just peered into the shadows. In her memory, this building had seen many incarnations. When she was a small child, it was still a winery. Then it had been renovated to provide a stable for her father's horse. Then it was just a great big junk-catcher.

But every Halloween, no matter what, the space had been transformed into the headquarters for the Haunted Vineyard. Theirs wasn't the biggest Halloween event in the area, or the most elaborate. Just a spooky maze in the vines, with fake tombstones and ghosts hanging from the trees. A few games, like pumpkin bowling, and a fortune-teller's tent. Candy, punch, a costume contest.

But the locals loved it, and everyone for miles around came every year. A couple of dollars bought you the whole evening—a real "steal," according to her father, who always resented the effort and the expense.

But her mother insisted, and it was one of the rare occasions when she won the argument. The tradition had begun back in her grandparents' day, and even Ben Watson didn't dare abandon it.

Another sign of how far he'd fallen, without his wife to steady him. Strangely, though, Hayley didn't feel any satisfaction at her father's decline. She just felt hollow.

It had been Halloween, as they were closing down the Haunted Vineyard, that she and Colby had first...

No. No more of that.

She flipped the switch on the inside wall, not sure what she'd see. More decay and disorder? But to her surprise, the overhead lights gleamed along a line of large, shiny machinery. A tractor, and a picker—those she recognized. The others were mysterious beasts with metal jaws and pincers and big, aggressive wheels.

She glanced back at Roland. "What is all this?"

"Your father went through a phase a couple of years ago. He decided he was tired of paying for labor. He thought if he bought all this equipment, he could do everything on the vineyard himself."

No more handpicking? No more human fingers on the vines, coaxing them to grow around the wires, orderly and aired out to avoid rot? She remembered that, right before she left, her father had given up the old zin vines, which grew in gnarled heads from a single trunk, and had opted for a more streamlined trellis. She'd been sad about that. She'd loved the way the hundred-year-old vineyard looked after it had been pruned, like rows of twisted, weather-beaten gray soldiers.

Still, in spite of his "updates," Foggy Valley, like most family-owned vineyards, had never been automated. Always handcrafted, from planting to harvest.

She couldn't quite comprehend it. She moved into the barn, and ran her hands over the undented, unstained, unmuddied surface of the nearest machine.

"This looks brand-new."

"Yes." Roland's low voice held a combination of pity and disapproval. "Realized, after he bought it, that of course he couldn't handle the vineyard by himself. He had to hire the labor after all, and these just went into storage." He paused. "I'm afraid that, up in the house somewhere, you're going to find the bills. All on credit, is my guess."

"Great." Hayley dropped her hand, suddenly exhausted at the thought of what she might find once she tackled the financial records. "Will I at least be able to sell these monsters for something, if I offer them along with the land?"

Roland shrugged. "Yes. Not much, but something. Market's really bad right now. Probably you know that."

"Yes." She shut her eyes. "Yes, I know."

"Peepaw! Peepaw!"

Elena's voice was high-pitched and urgent. She so rarely spoke a word that Hayley's eyes flew open. She started immediately to move in Elena's direction, fearful that something was wrong.

The little girl was tugging at her grandfather's hand. Her black curls bounced as she wriggled, trying to get his attention. But her face was alight—she was excited, not distressed.

"Peepaw, look!" She pointed toward the dirt road they'd taken to get to the winery building. "Look!"

Hayley looked, as they all did. Purring slowly down the road, its movement so sleek it didn't even seem to disturb the dirt, came a black sedan, its tinted windows spangled with sunlight.

Its understated elegance looked so out of place here, in this unkempt corner of the property.

The sedan came to a stop right in front of them, inches from the golf cart, half blocking its path. Elena's mouth dropped open, and she reached up to clutch Hayley's hand, too.

In the silence, an elderly man in a uniform unfolded himself from the front seat, as erect as a retired military general, and touched his cap in Hayley's direction.

"Ms. Watson? Mrs. Malone would like to speak to you, if it's convenient."

What on earth? Was this really the infamous Angelina Malone, Colby's grandmother? Hayley was shocked, but some detached part of her mind found the moment intensely ridiculous. In fact, she almost laughed out loud. It was like the scene in a film, when the mobster arrives, all silky and dangerous, to let you know what will happen if you don't pay up.

Except, she didn't owe the Malones anything.

Quite the opposite, which she'd gladly explain to this haughty, interfering matriarch if the woman insisted. She'd never met Angelina Malone back when she dated Colby. She'd never been considered good enough to take home to the famous Malone family events. So she certainly wasn't going to be ordered into the woman's luxury car now, for God only knew what kind of discussion.

She allowed a silky smile of her own. "I'm sorry," she said, icily polite, "but I'm afraid it's not convenient at all."

For a moment, the old man seemed to be at a loss, which felt good. Bet that was the first time anyone had ever told Angelina Malone to take her grand manner and stuff it.

Hayley started to turn away, toward the winery building. But out of the corner of her eye, she saw the sedan's back door open, and she paused, curious. She watched as an older woman stepped out.

At first glance, all Hayley could really absorb was a vague impression of confidence and good taste. Then she looked closer, and she registered how lovely this woman was, with the kind of ageless beauty a painter would want to capture on canvas. Healthy white hair framed a heart-shaped face that wore its lines with pride. The woman's eyes weren't blue like Colby's. They were a deep, chocolate-brown, but they were the same shape as her grandson's. They held the same hint of humor and intelligence.

Even more surprisingly, Angelina didn't drip diamonds or lace. She wore a sensible pair of khaki pants, a simple gold sweater belted at her trim waist, and… tennis shoes.

How could this be? Where was the haughty matriarch? Where was the overbearing, uncaring bitch who had swept into Hayley's house seventeen years ago and exploded her world?

"Hello, Hayley," the woman said, her voice neutral. Careful, but not unkind. Her gaze was unsettling, as if she already comprehended a hundred things about this moment that even Hayley herself wasn't sure she understood. "I'm Angelina. Colby's grandmother."

Hayley tried to find her bearings. "Yes," she said, still polite. "I know."

"I'm sorry to interrupt," Angelina went on, acknowledging Roland and Elena with polite smiles, too. "I wouldn't if it weren't important. But first…I suppose I should say that I completely understand that you probably don't want to talk to me."

"You do?"

"Of course." She seemed fully at ease, as if she didn't care one iota that she had an audience for this awkward exchange. "I wouldn't want to talk to me, either, if our positions were reversed."

"Then what— I can't imagine why, after all these years—"

The older woman shook her head. "Don't worry. I haven't come here to offer an apology. An apology would be worthless. Worse than worthless. The damage is done, and words can't undo it. But even more important, it would be insincere. When I visited your father that night, I was protecting my grandson, and, if the circumstances were the same, I'd do it again."

"I see." Hayley had to take three deliberate breaths before she could trust herself to speak. "Well, that's… frank."

Angelina smiled again. "I'm generally frank. It saves time and minimizes misunderstanding."

"Oh, I don't think we misunderstand each other, Mrs. Malone. I think I've always understood exactly how you felt about the situation."

Angelina mused over that for a few seconds. She tilted her head, as if she wanted to see Hayley from every angle.

"You've grown very beautiful," she said suddenly. "I suspected you would. And you don't seem to have become as bitter as I feared you might, given everything that happened. I'm very glad to know that."

"I don't think you know the first thing about me, Mrs. Malone." Hayley lifted her chin. "And, as I said,

I can't imagine why you're here. We share nothing but the past—and we can't change that."

"No, sadly, we can't. I learned that lesson when my son and his wife died, leaving their three sons in my care. But we can acknowledge that the events of the past were real, that they were important and that they caused pain. Only then can we try to move beyond it."

Hayley made an impatient sound under her breath. "Move beyond it to what?"

"To the business at hand." Angelina straightened to her full height. She wasn't tall, but she was imposing. "Diamante would like to create its own custom wine, a private label. As I remember, the zinfandel made from Foggy Valley grapes was special."

Hayley tried to think of a response. The owners of Diamante, more than anyone, knew how far this vineyard had fallen. All she could say was, "Yes. Very special. Once."

Angelina nodded. It was amazing how much she seemed to both communicate and comprehend without using many words. "Well, I think it can be special again. I understand that you inherited the property from your father, and that you plan to sell it. I'm here, Hayley, because we would like to buy your vineyard."

CHAPTER SIX

HE SHOULD HAVE known Hayley would bring body-guards.

When Colby arrived at Foggy Valley that Friday morning, at least ten minutes early for their appointment to tour the property, he found Hayley already outside. She was flanked by her real-estate agent, Greta Kinyon from over in Headley, and her dad's former vineyard manager, Roland Eliot.

Between them, Hayley stood as straight as a tin soldier. "Hello," she said, her voice chilly. She clutched a blue sweater in her hands, and she appeared to be addressing a ghost about two inches to his left.

"Morning," he responded casually, encompassing the whole group so he wouldn't make her nervous. He didn't risk eye contact, any more than she had. Later, maybe…if she thawed out during the tour.

Greta, in contrast, hugged him without inhibition. She was an old friend of Red's. Red did all the real-estate scouting and acquisition for Diamante, and he was gregarious, so he knew almost every agent within a hundred miles north or south of San Francisco.

Greta was terrific. About thirty, auburn hair, curvy below the neck and sharp as hell above. She'd even been Red's lady of the month once, a couple of years ago.

Hayley turned her face away from the hug, as if she'd

caught them having sex in the road. Mentally, Colby shook his head. This wasn't going to be easy—not that he'd expected it to be. How exactly did a person go about building a bridge across seventeen years of mistrust?

Well, you probably didn't start with Nana Lina. He'd been surprised, and not particularly happy, to discover that his grandmother had asked Sidney to drive her out here yesterday. He had a feeling that visit had set him back a lot. Any fool could see that Nana Lina wasn't ever going to be Hayley Watson's favorite person.

And Nana Lina wasn't a fool. So what exactly had she been up to?

"I needed to see the girl," Nana Lina had responded tartly when he questioned the visit. "We had to get some things straight. And we did. She's no mindless bimbo, thank God."

He had raised one eyebrow. "You thought I could have fallen in love with a mindless bimbo?"

He hadn't meant to say *love*. Nana Lina pretended she hadn't heard the word, and simply waved the logic aside.

"You were eighteen," she said, as if that settled it. "And you're a Malone. You boys are just like your father, and your grandfather, too, for that matter. You're all pushovers for bimbos, until the right woman finally comes along."

For Colby, of course, it had worked the other way around. The right woman had come along first, and when he lost her, he'd settled for a lifetime of second-best.

Still, he wondered whether Nana Lina's trip to Foggy

Valley might have been a subtle attempt to do a little matchmaking. She ordinarily stayed a mile away from their love lives, but this time…

This time was obviously different.

The property was so much smaller these days it hardly took much time to see it. An hour later, Greta, Hayley, Colby and Roland had inspected most of the land, vines and outbuildings, either on golf carts or on foot. Hayley explained that she wasn't ready to show the main house yet, which was fine, because he had no intention of living here.

If they bought, maybe they'd let the new manager move in. Either way, it could wait.

They'd already viewed the pinot acres, and the ridiculous shed full of unused, overpriced equipment that Ben must have bought one day when he wasn't getting enough oxygen to his brain.

As he dutifully made a list of everything in the old barn, he allowed himself no editorial comments. But Greta had wisely suggested that the vineyard could be sold with or without the machinery. Same with the house—sale could go through, with or without. Hayley hadn't said anything.

Now they were headed downhill on foot, through the remaining zinfandel blocks. At the base of the hill lay the old manager's house, which marked the end of the Foggy Valley land. No fog this morning, so it presented a homey sight, with smoke puffing out of the chimney, drifting away onto the chill blue October sky.

Nicer by far, actually, than the fancy house above them. Ben had sold the wrong piece. The sun slid down the hill like warm honey, and pooled in the red, gold and brown leaves of Roland's much-healthier vines.

Throughout the tour, Hayley and Roland had walked a little ahead. They stayed close enough that they could answer questions if they absolutely had to, but far enough away to discourage conversation. Colby had ambled behind with Greta. They spent at least half their time discussing his younger brother's transformation from playboy to almost-married man.

At the bottom of the hill, the tour was over. The four of them finally came face-to-face.

Greta smiled. "Well? Questions?"

Yeah—what the hell had Ben Watson been thinking? This sweet piece of earth, with its luscious grapes, rolling hills, fertile flats rimmed in ancient trees… It had almost been neglected to death.

But those were words that had to remain unspoken. Colby took out his phone. "I assume you won't mind if I bring someone out to take soil samples?"

Greta glanced at Hayley before answering. "No, that's fine. Of course. We'd expect that."

"And what about contracts?" Colby made sure Hayley saw that this question was for her. "Do you know how much of the yield is committed to wineries already?"

She flushed. Maybe from the heat. Maybe because there were no contracts. He could imagine that, given how Watson had let this pretty little vineyard go to hell.

"No, I'm sorry," she said. "I don't have those figures yet. I'm still working through the paperwork in the house. My father's filing system wasn't—particularly well organized."

"No problem. I guess that means you'll be staying around a while, then? To sort things out? So if I have more questions, I can give you a call?"

Her eyes widened. He knew what she was thinking—this was a little obvious. But he didn't have time for subtlety. He needed time alone with her. There was so much he needed to know, not just about the vineyard, but about her.

About the baby.

"You can always call Greta, of course," she said slowly.

"No. I'd really like to discuss things with you." He added a smile. "You've been gone a long time, but you still know the vineyard better than anyone."

"Oh, well, Roland knows—"

"No." No smile this time, but his voice wasn't aggressive, just firm. "We're serious about offering on the vineyard, Hayley."

She looked skeptical, perhaps with reason. "Serious" about offering might be an overstatement. At the last Diamante family meeting, they'd discussed the possibility of making an offer on Foggy Valley, but no final decision had been reached. No one but Nana Lina had been crazy about the idea.

She had pointed out that she was the only one who had ever tasted Foggy Valley Zinfandel in its prime. And of course, Nana Lina *was* Diamante. If she wanted to buy the vineyard, they'd buy it. If she didn't…

Then Colby would talk her into it.

Looking at Hayley's narrowed eyes, Colby wondered just how high she might set the price, now that she knew exactly who her bidders were. He supposed this was where he'd discover whether she was really as indifferent as she said—or whether she harbored enough bitterness to relish the idea of squeezing the Malone family for a few extra grand. Payback, maybe? In its most literal sense?

But that kind of thing wasn't in Hayley's nature.

Was it?

He studied her, trying to decide whether her changes were window dressing—or bone deep. As a fully grown woman, she'd become downright gorgeous, but then she'd always been fantastic. Creamy skin, light blue eyes, and a pink mouth mobile enough to tell him she still knew how to laugh. And the body—she hadn't changed much there, either, even after all these years. Slim as a teenager, with long legs and mouth-watering curves. More curves...

Her hair was still trapped in that complicated braid thing, but the wind was working hard to spring a few curls free, and the sunbeams fired off the gold and copper strands.

That was all merely the packaging, though. What was really going on now, inside her head? Or her heart...

The poise in her posture, the placid expression on her features, the restraint in her manner—those were new, and they made analyzing her difficult. Used to be, everything she felt had been telegraphed in her flushed cheeks and her rapid chatter.

With a stab, he suddenly remembered how he'd wait for her in the woods, and she'd come dancing in, smelling of sunshine and grapes, sparkling with some silly new idea.

"Let's go to Italy," she'd say as she threw herself into his arms. "Or Greece. Yes, Greece. Somewhere glamorous. Can we, Colby? Anywhere!"

What he wouldn't give to see that smile again.

"So what do you think?" He held her gaze without letting go. "Can we do business together? Or is negotiating with me directly a problem? Would it be too…?"

He let the sentence die off, knowing it sounded a little like one of the dares he'd issued in the old days— *bet you can't climb this taller tree, eat this bigger burger, strip all the way down and skinny-dip in Larkin's pond.* A year older than she was, and puffed up with the pride of a healthy eighteen-year-old male, he'd loved to play macho and egg her on.

And here he was doing it again, as if he were still eighteen. *I dare you… Are you afraid? Too scared to spend even that much time alone with me?*

First she frowned, as if she might dismiss the challenge as immature nonsense. Which, of course, it was. But then she bit her lower lip and almost imperceptibly squared her shoulders, a set of movements he remembered well. It meant she was about to call his bluff.

"It's no problem at all," she said. "In fact, why don't you bring your brothers, too? It'll be just like old times."

WHEN HAYLEY FIRST HEARD that Red Malone had taken over real-estate investments for Diamante, and her initial meeting would be one-on-one with him, she could hardly believe her ears.

In her mind, Red was still fifteen years old. Colby and Matt had called him *runt,* though he was only a year younger than Matt. Something about being the baby of the family, she supposed. But they always agreed to let him tag along, even though he had an annoying habit of sneaking up on Hayley and Colby and barking, "What the *hell* is going on here, son?" in his deepest voice. He'd laugh himself sick when they jumped apart, rearranging clothes and hair.

But, once her brain adjusted, and calculated that Red would be thirty-two now, not to mention that she'd heard he was about to become a husband and adoptive father, she decided she didn't mind. She'd always liked Red. He loved to horse around, but he had a sweet streak. Sometimes, when she and Colby fought, he'd been the one to smooth things over.

In fact, of all the people from her past, she probably would enjoy seeing him the most.

She'd chosen neutral territory for the meeting—Homespun, a small restaurant she'd noticed in downtown Ridley. Half bakery, half café, the smells that wafted through its doors were fabulous. Even better, Homespun had opened only a few years ago, in the storefront that used to be the hardware store. Long after her time. No memories to distract her.

All in all, she was actually looking forward to the meeting. So when she walked past the big front window and saw Colby sitting at a table for four, *all alone,* she was even angrier than she should have been.

Of all the cheap ploys...

Shoving her file of papers beneath her arm so sharply her armpit stung, she marched into the crowded café. The warm, yeasty scents of freshly baked rolls and cookies insinuated themselves into her senses, almost as if they urged her to calm down. But she refused to soften and made a beeline for his table.

"Why, Red Malone," she said drily. "You certainly have changed."

Colby pushed back his chair and stood, one side of his mouth tilted up in a half smile. "Sorry," he said. "Red got held up over in Headley. I told him I'd take over till he could get here."

She sat, ignoring his gentlemanly hand on the back of her seat, and scraped the wooden chair up to the table sharply. He sat, too, but with more restraint, watching her curiously. "He sent his apologies. It really was unavoidable."

"He doesn't have to apologize to me." Taking a breath, she placed the file between her knife and fork, then folded her hands over them. "This was all a ruse, wasn't it? The whole Red thing? Maybe even the whole vineyard thing. It was just a ruse to get me here. With you. Alone."

"Alone?" He tilted his head and took in the packed restaurant. They were literally less than two feet from filled tables all around them. On one side, a family with four boys was doing something raucous that seemed to involve toy soldiers bombing chocolate-chip cookies.

"We're hardly alone," he said. "But... Actually, no. There's nothing bogus about it."

She raised her eyebrows.

He made an exasperated sound. "Why should I go to the trouble of setting up a ruse? I thought we had an agreement. If I'd wanted to talk about the sale over lunch, instead of Red, would some kind of trick have been required?"

"No. But that's my point. I would have been glad to… I mean, I wouldn't… I mean, I don't want to—" She stopped, suddenly aware that she wasn't sure how to finish the thought. She was off track, and this wasn't the real issue at all.

Something about sitting here, only inches from a man she hadn't expected to meet again in this lifetime, was rattling her brain. She stared unseeingly at the children next to them, until she caught the youngest one, a boy of about three, staring back. His scrunched-up mouth said he thought she might be one of the strangers his dad had warned him about.

She turned her attention back to Colby. "The point is, I don't have time to waste playing games. I need to sell the vineyard as soon as possible. If you're really interested in launching a Diamante label, and you'd like to consider Foggy Valley, that's great. You can have all the lunch meetings you need."

He smiled. "But?"

"But if you're just posing as a buyer because you think it'll give you a chance to ask me questions about…about the past, well, then, we need to put an end to the vineyard charade right now."

He gazed at her a few seconds before responding. He toyed with a cup of coffee he must have ordered before she arrived. The china had a red stripe around the rim, matching the checkered tablecloth. The walls were a soft, pastel green. And every breath she took still smelled of wonderful spices and butter and warm wheat.

Nice place—just wrong company.

Finally he spoke. "What if it's both?"

"Both?"

"Yes. Both. Diamante is seriously interested in your vineyard and I also want a chance to talk to you about—as you put it—the past."

She must have scowled instinctively, because she saw the little boy at the next table scowl back at her, and hold up his three-inch toy battleship as if in warning. She tried to arrange her face into a less-threatening expression, but she wasn't sure how successful she was, because even Colby's eyes hardened.

"Look, Hayley, you dropped quite a bombshell on me the other night, about losing the baby. Everything I've always believed about what happened to our child—you turned upside down. And then…nothing. No explanation, no details, no…nothing. So if you're asking whether I have a private agenda here, whether I'm planning to use the business deal to create an opening for the personal questions, then the answer is yes."

"You admit it?"

"Of course. But be fair. What alternative do I have?" He leaned back in his chair, running his hand through his hair, mussing the waves so that they looked even more attractive. If that was possible. "It's not exactly as if you're issuing invitations to come up to Foggy Valley and chat."

She hesitated, surprised by his quiet intensity, and his candor. She'd been ready for a clever comeback. The Malone brothers were notoriously sardonic, masters of one-liners and nonanswers. If they didn't want to be pinned down, you could ask questions all day and never get a straight response.

So this answer, which didn't seem to hold any slippery subtext, caught her off guard.

Buying time, she watched the family with the boys as they stood and tried to clear the table and gather all their things. The mom and dad were laughing, in spite of the mess and chaos and the boys still bombing everything they could see.

She wondered if the Malone family had been like that, when Colby, Matt and Red were young. When she found out she was pregnant, her first thought had been how lovable a baby with Colby's genes would be. The very first—even before she asked herself what her father would say.

Naive little idiot that she was, she'd even imagined holding that warm, pink infant, staring down adoringly into his Malone-blue eyes...then looking up to see her husband, Colby, staring adoringly at her.

"Why is it so important to you?" She shook her head. "You know the basic facts. Do the details really matter all that much?"

"Yes."

"But I've told you...I've explained that I never talk about it. It took a long time, but I've finally put it behind me." She fidgeted with the papers, making her knife and spoon clank together. "Do you think you have the right to ask me to revisit it, just to satisfy your curiosity?"

"The right?" His blue eyes were very dark. "No."

She frowned. "Then why should I? You certainly had the chance, seventeen years ago—"

He put his hand on the back of her wrist. It wasn't a

calming touch, or an insistent one. It was merely a connection, a request that she really hear him.

"Because you're a better person than I am. You always were. I was a bastard, and a fool, and I betrayed you. You have the *right* to take whatever revenge you like. But I don't believe you're hard-hearted enough to look me in the eye and tell me the baby is none of my business."

She lifted her chin. "No?"

"No. I knew you, remember? Maybe better than anyone did. I don't believe you could have changed that much."

She put her hands in her lap, because the white crescents around her clenched fingers so clearly revealed her tension. And because his fingers were branding her skin.

"You'd be surprised," she said softly, "how much a loss like that…can change a person."

He didn't speak. He wasn't the type to beg. She wondered what it had cost him, emotionally, to expose as much vulnerability as he already had. It wasn't the Malone way.

She couldn't think what to say. She couldn't meet his eyes, either, so she let her gaze roam the restaurant. Around them, every table was full, except where the little boys had just been, and the whole space bustled with conversation and laughter. Young and old seemed to flock here, and eat hearty. She watched the customers checking out. Most of them had bakery bags, as well. The food must be wonderful.

She thought about going up to the counter and ordering something, but the line was so long. A couple of families, a few women taking their time and several people looking at their watches, as if lunch break was almost over.

She'd been gazing at the line so casually, her mind half somewhere else, that she only dimly registered a tall, broad-shouldered man with golden hair walking through the front door, heading out into the street. A rush of goose bumps along her arm told her even before her eyes did. The man looked a lot like Greg.

That was impossible. She was just skittish, that was all. He was already back in Florida, remember? His service had said so.

Still, she looked out the big window, quickly. The sidewalks were busy, but the man apparently hadn't turned in that direction. No one fitting that description walked past the glass.

Still edgy, she glanced around the restaurant, looking for where the empty tables might be. It wasn't a huge restaurant, but it was quite crowded. Could Greg have been here, sitting nearby, maybe even watching her— all without her being aware of him?

Most of the tables were still full. The table where the family of boys had sat was empty, of course. And the one just beyond that…

Her heart seemed temporarily to stop.

Greg had a strange habit, when he ate at restaurants. To signal the waiters that he was finished, he stacked his utensils on top of each other, knife on the bottom, fork on knife and spoon at the top. The half-empty plate she stared at right now was stacked exactly like that.

Her heart began to thump so loudly she wondered if Colby could hear it. *Calm down,* she told herself. It was a coincidence, that was all. Stacked silverware was quirky, but it wasn't exactly as conclusive as a fingerprint.

She was just spooked by his showing up the other day. And generally on edge because coping with her past was so stressful.

"Hayley?"

She looked back at Colby, swallowing hard, as if she'd just awoken from a trance. He was waiting for an answer, wasn't he? What was the question?

Oh, yes, of course. He wanted to know whether she'd talk with him privately, whether she'd tell him all about the baby.

She wondered what he would do if she said no again. She wondered whether he'd just take what was left of his pride and move on. Where, exactly, were the limits of his investment in this?

Suddenly, his cell phone beeped. He lifted it, tilting it for better light, and read something on its screen.

"It's Red," he said, swiping the message away without responding. He glanced up at her. "He's not going to be able to get here after all. But don't worry. He's got all the numbers, and all the right questions, so I won't try to take his place. He'll reschedule, sometime when it's convenient for you."

Relief flooded through her. She could leave, right now, before she…

Before she what? She didn't really know what she feared she might do. But her deepest instincts told her she wasn't ready to spend this much time alone with Colby. His voice, his gaze, even the tousled waves of his hair, shining blue-black in the reflected light from the window…

His presence affected her so much more than she would have imagined it would. She could find her balance, eventually. She simply wasn't strong enough, yet. She needed a little more time, that was all.

He set his phone on the table. "So, as you can see, you're free to go. Right now, if you want. I won't try to stop you. But will you promise me that you'll at least think about what I said?"

She felt him willing her not to leave, but she had to. She had to call Greg's office again—and this time she wouldn't accept the service's word for his whereabouts. She'd insist on talking to him herself.

And then, because her nerves were jangling from head to toe, she had to be alone, so that she could figure out what all these feelings really meant. And how to make them go away.

"All right," she said. "I'll think about it."

She gathered her papers and her purse. She stood. He stood, too, and she remembered the lovely manners his parents, and grandparents, had drilled into all the boys. They were cocky and wild, and thought girls had been invented for their pleasure, like milk shakes, or surfing. They sailed the *MacGregor* all day, forgot to call and hated to wait for anything.

But they also opened doors, noticed your earrings, sent flowers for silly anniversaries, like the first time they had watched you sleep. They whispered poetry while they trailed kisses down your spine and made you forget that it was wrong to be there, your naked breasts pressed against the hay in your father's barn.

The hot-cold, good-bad paradox had been irresistible, back then.

And maybe, heaven help her, it still was.

She had taken about two steps from the table before she turned.

"Tomorrow morning I'll be helping Roland set up the Haunted Vineyard," she said. "We'll probably be through by two. If you'd like, come up to the house then. Come alone. I'll do my best to answer your questions."

CHAPTER SEVEN

COLBY HAD NEGLECTED Diamante business for days now, so he spent the entire morning at the office, focused like a fiend, and batted out about a week's worth of work in six hours.

Matt and Red, who were chatting in the conference room over coffee, exchanged the smirking "get *him*" look as he came through to grab some files, but he ignored them. He couldn't explain it, but he buzzed with anticipation, just thinking about this afternoon with Hayley.

It wasn't excitement, exactly. He had a feeling that the meeting would be difficult at best—and possibly downright painful. She'd be resentful, and the memories she'd have to relive would be rough. In some ways, he felt like a jerk for making her do it.

But he couldn't help himself. She wouldn't remain in California long—he could feel her emotionally straining to get away already. This might be his only chance, and he had to grab it. He'd waited so long for answers. He had to know as much as she would tell him.

Just before one o'clock, he packed up. As he left the office, he dropped about two-dozen folders on his assistant Francie's desk, complete with instructions for who to call and which forms to file. She probably already knew that her email inbox was overflowing with other little tasks, as well.

But she was a marvel, and wouldn't be the least bit fazed. Though she had an ogre's temper and made coffee that tasted like muddy acid, their office had never been run so well. He wondered what he'd do when she finally got her law degree and left him.

When he told her he'd be gone for the day, she didn't look surprised.

"Good luck," she said as he punched the button for the elevator. He wasn't sure what she meant by that, since he hadn't told anyone where he was going. He glanced back at her, and she just chuckled and shook her head.

"Think I haven't ever seen you in courting mode before, boss?"

"I'm not—" he started to say, but a chortle came out of Matt's office, and the elevator arrived, so he merely frowned and didn't bother to finish. "And here I was, just thinking I'd miss you when you finally passed the bar." He entered the elevator and pressed Down. "*If* you pass the bar."

The doors closed on her laughter, but her words followed him all the way to the parking lot. He wasn't courting, damn it.

It wasn't that he wouldn't welcome the chance to romance Hayley Watson again. Something about her had always activated every male hormone in his body, and still did. But he didn't have any illusions about his chances with her.

Zero to subzero.

Even so, as he skimmed up the 101 north, forcing

himself to stay somewhere near the speed limit, he realized he hadn't felt this edgy in years. Or this alive.

He'd misjudged the early-afternoon traffic, being used to rush hour, and realized he was going to get there before two. He cut off the highway and wound through a more scenic route toward the vineyard, which lay just a little west of the Russian River Valley. He pulled over to get gas, and flipped the top down. After that, he drove sensibly, appreciating the view and the crisp October breeze, which stung his cheeks pleasantly and seemed to clear his head a little.

By the time he reached Foggy Valley, he felt more in control. He rolled slowly past Roland's house at the foot of the hill, which was a good decision, since clearly the group work session for the Haunted Vineyard was still underway.

Roland and one of the teenage volunteers were hanging the silver crescent moon swing from a nearby live oak, and a little girl danced around them in circles, her fists jammed against her chin in barely restrained excitement. She clearly was begging to be allowed to sit on the sparkling seat.

Amazing that the silver moon had lasted all these years. Though the venue had moved, the traditions continued.

Colby let his gaze scan the vineyard. Tombstones popped out from between the posts, as usual, and…

Yes. His heartbeat quickened like a teen's. There she was…bent over at the waist, her head invisible under the vines as she wove the purple fairy lights along the vines. His body stirred uncomfortably. What a view! Once, he'd had to explain a few facts to a drunken jerk over in Ridley who had told Hayley she had the "sweetest ass in six counties." Luckily, Matt had been along that night, and the sight of two angry Malone brothers, particularly fit that summer because of all the surfing, had been enough to make the guy apologize.

Their parents hadn't allowed fighting, under any circumstances, for any reason, and Nana Lina and Grandpa Colm reinforced those rules when they took over. But the jerk didn't know that. For the most part, guys like him were easily intimidated, so having two brothers as backup usually did the trick.

He nudged the car into Park.

"Hi," he called. "Need any help?"

She tried to straighten abruptly, but her hair caught in one of the upper branches of the vine. Roland's vines were old-school, head-trained and spear-pruned, as all the Foggy Valley vines used to be, before old Watson got so greedy.

She dropped the long strings of lights and twisted, trying to free herself, but her hair was tied back in a tight ponytail, and nothing wanted to budge. He killed the engine and got out to help.

By the time he reached her, she was bent into a right angle at the waist, the vines seeming to grow out of her head. Her cheeks blazed a sharp pink and her eyes were squeezed tight and furious.

"Hold still," he said, biting back a grin. He ducked around to get a look at the back, where the problem was. "I think we're going to have to lose the ponytail."

"Okay," she said between her teeth. "Thanks."

He had to move in very closely, and stoop to reach the right level. Once there, he worked quickly, slipping the elastic band over the mass of curls. She sighed as some of the pressure loosened, and he tunneled his fingers into the thick silk until he found the tangle that was causing all the trouble. He massaged it free, until he was down to the last few strands, which he had to tear away from the branch.

She straightened with a moan of relief. "Thank you," she said. She reached up and rubbed the spot herself, then tried to comb the length of the messy curls with her fingers. "I'm sorry—is it two already? I must have lost track of time, because there's so much—"

Suddenly she seemed to notice how close he stood, and she stopped midsentence, her mouth slightly open. Her pink cheeks drained instantly to pale. In the spotlight of the sun, her blue eyes were clear and prismatic…and intensely aware of him.

He was close enough to smell the shampoo she'd used this morning. Roses, or cherries…something red and clean and sweet. She blinked, as if dazed.

He was close enough to kiss her. He'd kissed her so many times among these vines that it felt natural to consider it. Without giving his common sense time to kick in, he cupped his hand around the back of her head and started to lean forward.

"Miss Hayley, Miss Hayley! Peepaw says to ask you if I can swing in the moon!"

The high-pitched sound came from one of the nearby rows. He heard light footsteps pattering toward them, and finally a little girl appeared, ducking between two crooked old vines to find them.

"Please," she said, her upturned features almost

burning with the intensity of her need. "Please, Miss Hayley, say yes!"

"Hi, sweetie!" Hayley rushed over, bent down and scooped the little girl into her arms. "Why does your peepaw want me to decide?"

The child apparently had just noticed Colby, and she instantly became subdued, burying her face in Hayley's neck. "Because," she said, her voice low and solemn. "It's in the tree. And you are the girl who sleeps in the treetops."

Hayley glanced at Colby. Was she wondering if he remembered what that meant? Or was she trying to gauge whether the child's interruption had annoyed him?

"All right," she said in a very matter-of-fact tone, turning her attention back to the little girl. "But I'll have to know a few things before I can decide. How far off the ground did your peepaw and the workers hang the swing?"

Without raising her head, Elena spread her arms out to show the distance—probably a couple of feet.

"Okay. And did he use very strong rope?"

The shining black curls bobbed in a vigorous "yes." Colby had to smile at that question. Unless Roland had changed the routine, on the night of the Haunted Vineyard, the swing would hold one of the teenaged volunteers, so the rope was intended to support at least three times Elena's weight.

"Okay," Hayley said again. "And do you promise to hold on very tightly, and be very careful, as the princess of the silver moon always must?"

More nodding. The girl had raised her head, though,

and was staring into Hayley's eyes with her own, shining dark ones.

"Good." Hayley smiled. "Then my answer is yes."

A squeal of delight greeted that, and Elena pressed her face hard against Hayley's cheek, puckering her rosebud lips in a childish kiss. Colby saw the irony, of course. It wasn't the kind of kiss he'd been offering, but it clearly was the kind Hayley preferred. Her smile deepened, and she hugged Elena tightly for a moment before putting her back on the ground.

"Peepaw! Peepaw! She said yes!" Elena's short legs churned through the row of vines as she skipped back to her grandfather.

They listened for several seconds, as the childish voice grew fainter. Then, squaring her shoulders, Hayley turned to Colby. "Let me just tell Roland that I'm leaving," she said. "You'll probably want to park the car up at the house. How about if I meet you there in five?"

Their moment had passed. But his thrumming body didn't seem to know that. He couldn't stop looking at her, couldn't stop wondering why all the years hadn't killed this feeling.

The breeze had picked up, and it tossed her curls around, lifting them into the air like golden fire, and then tickling them across her cheeks and lips. She grimaced, peeling them away.

"Hayley," he said softly. She looked at him, but he couldn't go on. This was the first time since she'd come back that he'd seen her with her hair loose, and the sight made his knees feel oddly weak.

It was as if someone had turned back the hands

of time. Surely he'd seen that ratty white sweatshirt before, drooping from that slim shoulder. Surely those were the same dark blue, clam-digger-length jeans, with the buttons that drove him crazy, because they took so long to thumb free.

"Yes?"

He got a grip on himself, just in time. "I just wanted to say… If you have more to do here, I understand. In fact, I'd be glad to pitch in. With two pairs of hands, we could probably get these lights up in no time."

The offer seemed to surprise her. She hesitated, and he could almost see her brain processing the possible implications of accepting his help. She even glanced over to Roland, halfway across the vineyard, as if he might be able to signal her some advice.

Finally she shook her head. "No, that's very nice of you, but we should stick to the plan." She even smiled a little. "If we cancel now, who knows if I'll get the courage to say yes another time?"

SHE KEPT THE STORY SHORT. No way she could get through it if she wallowed in all the terrible, bloody details.

When they both got up to the house, she made coffee, and then they moved into the living room, drinking, or at least holding the mugs, while she talked. The room wasn't fully sorted out yet—she still hadn't even forced herself to open her father's rolltop desk. The lawyer had a copy of the trust, and there was no life-insurance policy, so she figured the creditors could wait a few days at least.

It wasn't as awkward as she'd feared, having Colby inside. He hadn't ever spent much time in the house, anyhow. It wasn't any fun here, with her beer-soaked father glowering at the television in his shorts and T-shirt, muttering occasionally about the something-something-goddamn-Malones. The few times Hayley had brought Colby over, her mother had driven them nuts, nervously offering one thing after another—Cokes, cookies, popcorn, chitchat—to compensate for her husband's lack of hospitality.

So, though her dad knew she dated Colby occasionally, he had no idea how far the relationship had gone. During his infrequent spurts of paternal concern, he loved to warn Hayley against getting involved with the Malones at all. They were, he said, the "chew 'em up and spit 'em out" kind of people.

Her mother had chosen her words more gently, but by the third summer, when she saw that Hayley kept letting Colby Malone come back, like some kind of migratory bird, she'd been worried enough to speak.

Her message had been about the same. "They don't really know how to value a girl like you," she would say. "They've always had too much. If you give him your heart, Hayley, he'll break it. He might not mean to, but he will."

The warnings had slid right over her, like river water flowing over a stone. What did they know of Colby—of the way his hands cherished her body, and his laughter warmed her heart? Look at her parents—they barely spoke, much less touched! What did they know of love, especially young love?

More than she did, as it turned out. The irony of that wasn't lost on her, even during the worst of the pain, in the horrible little hospital.

Colby took the armchair, and he listened without interruption, even managing to keep his face impassive. He had always been a very good listener, making her feel that she was the only girl in the world.

She spelled out the basic facts—the beating, the midnight flight, the psychedelic nightmare at an E.R. in a tiny town in Nevada, where her mother gave a fake name and some cockamamie story to explain the injuries. Then, abruptly out of energy, she stopped cold.

She took a long swig of her lukewarm coffee. And then she waited, feeling too emotionally limp to care how the story had sounded. She'd told the truth, no evasions or sugarcoating, either for him or for her.

It was all she could do. If he wanted more, he would have to ask specific questions.

At first, he didn't. He set down his mug on the end table and stood, as if being completely immobile all that time had been a struggle, and his muscles called for release. He walked to the bookcase, and touched one of the titles blindly. He started to take the book out, but seemed to realize how absurd that was, and shoved it back. His hand gripped the edge of the shelf, and he momentarily bowed his head.

Still spent, she gazed at the bookshelves, too, and wondered disconnectedly what her father had done with her mother's figurines. There'd been a beautiful shepherdess, whose dress was made of some magical combination of lace and porcelain that would shatter at the slightest touch. And a little dog, with his front paws in the air. And a woman stretched languidly across a bed. Gen had called that one "Sleeping Beauty."

Hayley wondered whether her father might have

smashed them all, when he awoke and found his family gone.

And then a strange, stray thought came to her. She wondered whether, when she decided to date Greg, she'd unwittingly been drawn to a man who had the capacity for violence in him, however deeply it might be buried. She always pitied women who came from abusive households and ended up replicating the drama with their husbands and lovers, drawn to violence like metal filings to a magnet.

Surely she couldn't have become one of those women?

She glanced out the window, watching the wind play with the leaves. Thank God she'd called Greg yesterday, and insisted on speaking to him. When the nurse caved in, and agreed to put him on the phone, Hayley had just hung up.

Childish, maybe. But if she hadn't been assured he was safely back in Florida, she'd probably see him hiding behind every zinfandel trunk. Last night was the first time she'd actually stayed at the house, and, even in her parents' bed, her sleep had been surprisingly dream-free.

Colby took a deep breath, and then he turned around. Every muscle in his face was so tight it almost made him look like a different person. He was hurting, and he might even be angry. But nothing in him hinted at aggression or violence.

Still…he'd managed to hurt her even worse, in his own way.

"I'm sorry," he said. "It's so useless to say so, and it's far, far too late. But I am. I'm so goddamn sorry."

"Yes." She nodded numbly. "Me, too."

He ran his hand over his brow, took another breath, then came back and sat again, but this time on the sofa, beside her. "What about you? Once you got help, were you okay? I mean, physically? Were there any long-term injuries?"

She took another sip of the coffee, just to wet her dry mouth. "My leg was in a cast for about eight weeks. And they had to take my appendix out—too much trauma in the abdominal area. Within a few months, though, I guess you'd say I was fine."

"What about—having children? Any permanent damage that would make it—difficult?"

She'd known he'd ask this question. And she knew why.

"The doctors always say they don't think so. There's some scarring, but they say it probably wouldn't interfere with normal..." She tried to remember their idiotic phrasing. "Normal reproductive function."

He frowned. "But you haven't...tried."

She laughed, but it didn't sound quite like laughter, somehow. "I'm not exactly sure what you're asking."

He didn't shrink from her brittle tone. In fact, he shifted closer, and turned slightly, so that he was facing her, his knees only a few inches away from her fingertips.

"I suppose I'm asking whether you've ever married. Whether you've ever had children—or tried to. Don't forget, I know very little about what's happened over these years. For all I know, you might have three ex-husbands by now. You might have left half-a-dozen children at home, while you came out to bury your past."

"No." She waved her hand, encompassing the various questions. "To all of that."

"Why not?"

She raised one eyebrow, a trick he'd taught her that last summer. "Are you hoping I'll say no man could ever measure up to my memories of you?"

"Hardly. I'd assume your memories of me are fairly unflattering. I'm asking because…" He shook his head and put his hand along the back of the sofa. He let his fingertips graze her shoulder. "Well, because if you had half-a-dozen children, that would make me happy."

Suddenly angry, she shifted out of his reach. "It would let you off the hook, you mean."

His black brows drew together, the closest a Malone ever came to showing he'd been hit. And within a split second, she felt petty, and disappointed in herself.

She had loved this man so much, once. Today might be the last time the two of them talked privately. She'd return to Florida soon, and chances were she'd never even see him again.

So, if she could just calm herself and be reasonable, this could be her chance to find a little peace. They were older, wiser, saner. He wasn't the Devil Colby of her dreams anymore. He was a grown man, with the maturity to offer a sincere apology for his sins. Surely they could find a way to be…

She almost thought *friends.* But then she remembered the sizzle that shot through her veins whenever she saw him. With a rush of dismay, she realized why she kept retreating behind a wall of pseudobitterness.

Because he *was* still the Devil Colby.

He still held the power to confuse her, to seduce her, to smash her hard-earned protective shell just by standing too close to her in a sun-drenched vineyard.

Or sitting beside her on the sofa.

"I'm sorry," she said, trying to rise above this new, uncomfortable awareness. "I don't mean to sound so bitter. I'm not, really."

He looked somber. "You have every right to be."

"No, really, I don't. I'm alive, and basically, I'm fine. But only because my mother and my sister made a terrific sacrifice to protect me. About a year after the miscarriage, I finally woke up and realized I had no right to wallow in self-pity. What about Gen? She is such an easygoing person, such a peacemaker, that she could probably have coexisted placidly with Dad forever, and never triggered his temper. But she got ripped out of her normal life, just because of me. For her sake, I had to pull myself together."

"You always were her guardian angel." He smiled, finally. He'd liked Genevieve. "How is she?"

"She's great. You wouldn't believe how grown up."

She relaxed against the sofa cushions for the first time since they'd entered the room. It felt a little odd, having this kind of cocktail-party small talk, but at least they were moving past the ugliness, one small step at a time. "We're still roommates, but she's found a guy. Any minute now, I expect to see her waltz in with a diamond on her hand."

This time his smile reached all the way to his eyes, and she still knew his expressions well enough to tell it was genuine. He'd always understood about siblings.

He'd never minded when Gen tagged along, any more than she'd minded about Red.

"Matt's married now, and Red will be soon," he said. "Why any woman would sign up for a lifetime of those two bums, I can't imagine. But they both found wonderful women. You'd like them."

She nodded politely. "I'm sure I would."

"Maybe, if you stay long enough, you'll meet them. Red is going to marry a woman from Windsor Bay. She's got a kid of her own, and they're already talking about having another. Matt's got two kids. I brought his daughter, Sarah, up here for the Haunted Vineyard last year, if you can believe that. She loved it."

"That's great." She could hear the hollow note in her voice, in spite of her best efforts to hide it. So strange, to think of those teasing, athletic, heartbreaker boys as family men. In a strange, irrational way, she felt…left behind. It was as if she'd been trapped in ice, while the rest of the world moved on.

But that wasn't true. She'd been building a decent life out of her new realities. Greg had been a terrible misstep, but many things had gone right. She'd found friendship, and fulfillment in her job, and even, once or twice, a pleasant, transient romance. And, in a few months, she'd finally have the ultimate prize, the reward for all her patience.

Just twelve weeks, give or take, and she'd have a family of her own. A future of her own.

"In fact, I'm pretty sure you will meet them," he said. "Red and Allison can't stand to be parted, so he's likely to bring her up when he comes to look at the property.

And Matt's wife, Belle, does PR for the company, so if you're here long enough, you'll undoubtedly—"

"I really don't think I will," she interrupted. She tried to smile, so that she didn't seem too curt. "They sound delightful, but I have to get back to Florida as quickly as possible."

He tilted his head. "Why?"

"I have a life there. I have a job."

"What do you do?"

"I…I manage a small chain of dress stores. The owners have been very generous already, giving me leave time to arrange things out here."

"*Dress* stores?"

He looked surprised. She knew it probably didn't sound like much, not to the Stanford-educated heir to a thriving business. She used to talk about becoming a lawyer, or a psychologist, or a vet. But that had mostly been to make Colby think she was special, nothing like her drunken father. Still, all through high school, she'd never let her grades slip, because she knew she'd need scholarships if she was ever going to have a chance.

A doctor, a psychologist, a vet. Who knew which dream might have lasted, if her life had gone as planned?

But it hadn't. By the time she could use her own name, and get admitted to any kind of college, her paycheck had been far too important to their household.

"Does that disappoint you?" She sat up straighter. "I didn't know you were that kind of snob, Colby. I like my job. I'm good at it."

"I'm sure you are. I'm just surprised because…well,

you never really did go in for dresses, as I recall. It's hard to climb trees in a dress."

It was true. She'd been a tomboy from the start, and even today she still virtually lived in jeans. How they'd giggled in the dark, as he tried to unbutton them! Thwarted and grouchy, he'd complained that the jeans were as good as a chastity belt. She knew then that he was accustomed to lying in the shadows with a different kind of girl, whose designer jeans unzipped with ease.

Remembering, she forced herself not to blush—not easy, since her fair skin registered every change in her feelings like a visual thermometer.

"Oh. Sorry." She shrugged. "I guess I'm just a little prickly about it."

"But…" He took a minute, eyeing her closely, as he seemed to search for the right words. "Seriously. It's a good job, but undoubtedly one you could duplicate here without too much trouble. Have you ever considered just…staying?"

She widened her eyes. "Here?"

He nodded. "Now that your father's gone, you don't have to sell the property if you don't want to. You could stay and run it yourself. It's still a sound vineyard, at the core. You know Roland would be glad to help."

"Oh, no." She shook her head firmly. "Definitely not."

"Why not? You loved this vineyard, just like your mother did. Gen didn't really care one way or another. She's probably fine in Florida. But not you."

Her head was still shaking. Had he so little imagination that he couldn't guess how much unhappiness this vineyard represented for her?

"No. I need to get home as soon as I can. There's nothing for me in Sonoma. Everything I care about is in Florida."

His gaze sharpened. "Everything like what? There is a guy, then? You're—serious about someone?"

"It's not a man. I was seeing someone recently, but we're not together anymore."

That didn't seem to surprise him. Why would it? He had changed girlfriends the way other guys changed the oil in their cars. At least, he had as a teen. And the sardonic way he'd talked about his brothers' marriages— he sounded like a guy who still thought, as he'd said all those years ago, that "the only difference between a wedding ring and a noose is the price."

"Okay. Not a man. Then what?"

She hesitated. She hadn't shared her news with anyone except Genevieve, and it seemed preposterous that Colby Malone should be the first outside person she trusted enough to tell.

But maybe it was time to open up, and maybe this was, after all, the perfect place to start. At least then he'd understand why nothing on this earth could prevent her from returning to Florida.

"I can't stay here. Not just won't. Can't." She brushed at her jeans, where a few bits of glitter from the silver moon had implanted themselves. "I've made a commitment. I've signed a legally binding contract, promising that I'll permanently live in Florida."

"Forever? No matter what?" He frowned, his gaze bewildered. "Who asks for a commitment like that? It's not even enforceable. Why on earth would you promise such a thing?"

"Because…" She took a steadying breath and lifted her gaze to his. "A few months ago, the daughter of one of my work friends found herself…unexpectedly pregnant. Anna is only seventeen, really sweet, a wonderful girl. But she just doesn't feel she's ready to bring up a baby."

His face was blank for a second. And then he opened his mouth. "God. Hayley." The words came out on a harsh breath.

She didn't let his obvious shock stop her. "Her mother knew that I had been— Well, she knew she could turn to me. It's been arranged since the very beginning, practically from the moment Anna found out. I've been paying for her medical care, and the papers are all drawn up and ready."

He hadn't even blinked. It was as if he'd turned to stone.

"I hope you'll be happy for me, Colby." She smiled, though her face felt stiff and unnatural. "Because in just about three months, I'm going to adopt a newborn baby boy."

CHAPTER EIGHT

GRETA KINYON'S MAIN office was over in Headley, but she had a satellite office in downtown Ridley. It wasn't large, but it was elegant and welcoming. Hayley felt right at home the minute she stepped inside.

Up till now, Greta had come out to Foggy Valley whenever they needed to talk, so this was Hayley's first visit. She was impressed. Nothing shoddy or cluttered, but also nothing sterile. People who wanted to buy vineyards probably were looking for warmth and life, and they found it here.

The marketing theme continued when Greta herself walked in. Dressed in a simple red suit, her merlot-tinted hair sleek and glossy around her face, she smiled as if meeting with Hayley was the highlight of her week.

She hugged Hayley like an old friend, though they had met only a week ago. "Thanks so much for coming my way this time. My Ridley staff doesn't work on Mondays, except Tim, who answers the calls from home. So I'm holding down the office alone today!" Greta motioned Hayley to a French provincial armchair facing her desk. "But I've got good news!"

Hayley sat, wishing she'd put on something dressier than her jeans for the occasion. "Really?"

Greta typed a bit, studied the screen and nodded.

"Yes. It's amazing. We haven't even listed the vineyard officially yet, and already we have three interested buyers!"

"Three?" Hayley cynically wondered whether it was mostly vultures gathering, assuming that a neglected vineyard inherited by an estranged daughter could be snatched up for a fraction of its worth.

Greta leaned back in her chair, twirling her pen and eyeing the computer screen with a satisfied look. "Yep. You know about Diamante, of course. But one of your neighbors called yesterday, a Mrs. Ellenton-Barnes. She specifically asked me to identify her to you, so that you'd know she was legit. She bought a few of your father's acres some years back, and had been hoping to buy more when they became available."

Well, that made sense. Hayley could imagine her father dangling the acres out like a carrot, keeping Mrs. Ellenton-Barnes on the hook. Given the state of his finances, he probably hadn't been far from carving up the property again, anyhow.

"And the third?"

Greta chewed thoughtfully on her lower lip, as she read over her notes. "The third is still a bit of a mystery. He called this morning. He seemed extremely interested, but I'm not sure he's quite what we're looking for. He asked a lot of questions about you."

Hayley's back stiffened. "About me?"

"Yeah, it's not uncommon for the buyers to want to know personal stuff about the seller, but it's rarely a good sign. Usually means they're trying to find out how desperate you are to unload the property. Most of the time, they'll come in with a lowball offer."

"Did you get his name?"

The minute she asked, Hayley felt uncomfortable. Probably real-estate agents weren't eager to share information like that, even if they had it.

She smiled apologetically. "Sorry. It's just—there's a guy I dated recently, back in Florida. He's being kind of…" What was the right word, a word that wouldn't make her look paranoid? "He's not handling our breakup well, and he's being a little pushy."

Greta frowned, and tapped her pen on the desk blotter. "Pushy like annoying? Or pushy like stalker?"

"Somewhere in between," Hayley responded honestly. "I mean, he's a normal person…and he's a well-respected doctor. So he's not a weirdo. But he showed up at the vineyard the other day, all the way from Orlando—which was fairly disturbing, since I hadn't even told him where I was going."

Greta's eyes widened. "Well, *yeah.*"

"I don't really think he'll do anything else. He could tell how angry I was. And he seemed to accept that he'd made a mistake. He's gone back to Florida now."

She decided not to mention the coincidence of the blond man and the strangely stacked utensils at Homespun the other day. The more she thought about it, the more she felt sure she'd imagined the whole thing.

"He could have been the caller this morning, I suppose," Greta said thoughtfully. She touched her mouse and scrolled a little, checking the screen. "Actually, he wouldn't leave a name or number, so I have no idea. He sounded maybe mid-to-late thirties? Deep voice. Educated, no accent. Nice enough, even when he realized I wasn't going to fork over any personal information."

Hayley's skin prickled. That was such a generic description, and yet, if she'd had to describe Greg, she might have used those exact words.

Greta typed a few notes into her computer, then turned to Hayley with an upbeat smile. "Good to know about him, anyhow. Always helps to be forewarned. But even if our third interested party is fake, we still have two nibbles." She put down her pen. "Well, the Malones are doing a lot more than nibbling. In fact, the only role Mrs. Ellenton-Barnes is likely to play here is spoiler."

"Spoiler?"

"You know, competition. Her interest might persuade the Malones to go higher."

Hayley shifted slightly, folding her hands in her lap. "Or bow out."

"Bow out?" Greta laughed merrily. "Not likely. I've been in this business long enough to know when a buyer is truly committed. Colby intends to own this vineyard. You could ask twice what it's worth, and I honestly think he'd write the check today."

Hayley wasn't so sure about that. "Wouldn't Mrs. Malone have something to say about that? And what about his brothers? Surely the Diamante money isn't Colby Malone's own personal piggy bank."

Greta's smile was closed-lipped, but oddly knowing. Hayley wondered what she had heard about Hayley's past.

She started to say something, but then, behind Hayley, the front door opened, and Greta's face lit up. "Speak of the devil," she said, and rose to greet her new visitors.

Hayley twisted in her chair. Devil, indeed. It was

Matt and Redmond Malone. They'd entered, laughing, and clearly in the middle of one of the fraternal ribbings she remembered so well.

"Yeah, well, if Belle finds out, you're a dead man," Red was saying. "Not that we'll miss you much, but…"

They stopped when they saw Hayley in the room. It was comical, really. They almost did a freeze frame just inside the door. She had no doubt that they recognized her instantly. Either she hadn't changed as much as she thought, or they'd already been given a description of what she looked like now.

It had been seventeen years since she'd seen them, too, of course. But, just as it had been with Colby, she didn't have an instant's doubt. Apparently the Malone men—even *married* Malone men—simply got better with age. Matt was easy to spot, because he'd inherited the darker coloring of the Italian side of the family. Red, with all the easy charm of a youngest child, was like a sunnier version of Colby—black Irish, with lustrous dark hair and deep blue eyes.

Both still had the suntans and muscles that said they hadn't given up surfing, and the twinkle in their eyes that said they still saw the world from that shared sardonic tilt.

She'd known them fairly well, back when she dated Colby. Matt and Colby had worked at the newly opened Diamante store in Ridley three summers running, learning the company ropes. And naturally Red tagged along.

Technically, they were under the supervision of a manager, but that was a joke. The manager understood what it meant to have Malone boys on the payroll, and besides, the man was only about twenty-five himself.

So there was always time to play. And always plenty of eager girls to play with.

Girls like Hayley.

Not likely their arrival here at Greta's office was a coincidence. It must have something to do with the sale of Hayley's property. So she stood politely and held out her hand.

"Hi, Matt. Red." From a distance, she admired her own aplomb. After a certain number of awkward reunions, she supposed anyone could start to get used to them. "Hayley Watson. It's been a long time."

"As if we didn't know!" Red winked at her. Always the most easygoing of the whole carefree clan, he came hurrying over. Ignoring her hand, he enveloped her in a hug. "It would take a lot longer than seventeen years for us to forget you, Hayley Watson."

Meeting Matt's gaze over Red's shoulder, Hayley felt herself blushing. "That's very sweet," she said, and extricated herself as gracefully as possible. Matt took his turn, though the hug he offered was more restrained, and easier to get out of.

Greta got her hugs next.

"You two here to pick up the Foggy Valley inventory list?" Greta flipped through the neat stack of documents next to her computer, found a stapled set of papers and laid it on her desk. "I emailed you a copy this morning, but I guess you haven't been to your office."

"No." Matt glanced at his watch. "We're on our way out to the vineyard right now. Colby's already there, with the soil specialist." He turned to Hayley. "He said he'd arranged it with you. I thought you'd probably be out there, working with them."

"Greta had some paperwork she needed me to sign. Anyhow, I don't know much about soil requirements, so I thought it might be better if I just got out of his way."

Matt smiled, but his intelligent eyes were fixed on her curiously, as if she were a puzzle, and he hadn't put all the pieces together yet.

"Can't say I blame you," Red said wryly, filling the gap. "I avoid him as often as I can, myself."

She wasn't sure how to respond. She'd never been as good as they were at the witty deflections that kept conversations from getting too serious.

Luckily, she didn't have to. Right then, Matt's cell phone rang. He shot Hayley and Greta an apologetic glance, then thumbed the "answer" tab and held it to his ear.

"Hey," he said, in his usual wry tone. "Stop nagging, Grandpa. Ten minutes. We're just stopping by Greta's to pick up—"

He broke off the sentence abruptly, and everyone could hear a male voice on the other end speaking firm and fast. Matt's expression never altered, but somehow Hayley gathered he wasn't getting good news. She thought of the two little children Colby had mentioned, and said a quick prayer that this call wasn't about either of them.

Red's gaze on his brother had sharpened, too. With that sixth sense they had about each other, he obviously knew something was up, as well. He pulled car keys out of his pocket and picked up the papers on Greta's desk, preparing himself to respond if needed.

Hayley heard Matt say only a few words. But they were ominous enough.

"Yes. When? How serious? Has someone called—" He caught Red's gaze and made a rotation with two fingers, clearly saying, *let's go.* "Okay. We'll be there in five."

When he ended the call, Hayley expected them to dash off, but instead Matt turned to her. His face was, for once, devoid of all teasing. She held her breath, wondering what this had to do with her. Had something happened at the vineyard?

Had something happened to Colby?

"You might want to come," Matt said, without bothering to sugarcoat. "That was Colby. A sudden thunderstorm moved through, and they've had a lightning strike out in the vineyard. Roland Eliot's barn is on fire."

CHAPTER NINE

HAYLEY SPED, BUT she simply couldn't cover the distance between Greta's office and the vineyard in less than twenty minutes. By the time she reached the Eliots' barn, with Red and Matt's car close behind, the drama was almost over.

All that remained was a hellish half hour of noise—the crackle of flames, the crash of falling boards, the tinkle of broken glass. The barking of orders, the roar of water. The weeping of a little girl who couldn't understand what was happening to her world.

At the end of those thirty minutes, the yellow-coated firefighters were still gushing long, glittering arcs of water onto the charred barn, but no longer trying to save it. Too late for that—now they were merely making sure it was truly extinguished.

A freak accident, they said. A lightning bolt had hit the roof of the barn, where it found a faulty electrical wire. After that, the gas cans inside had apparently finished the job.

The blazing barn had caught the trees, and the trees spit a few sparks over onto the roof of the Eliots' house. The firefighters had extinguished it quickly, but in the rooms closest to the barn, smoke and water damage were pretty bad.

Obviously aware that she'd be wrestling with the aftermath for hours, Miranda asked if Hayley would take Elena up to the big house. The little girl had witnessed enough today.

Hayley was glad to. She needed to start clearing some rooms. She had told Miranda that the little family could stay with her for a couple of days, until their house was fit to live in again.

But freeing up enough space was going to take a lot of work. Her mind raced, trying to think where she could put everything that her father had piled into the bedrooms.

She hadn't talked to Colby since she arrived—though she knew he was still there, and had glimpsed him once or twice, moving furniture, pulling away smoldering boards, she'd been too busy tending Elena to chat. But now, as she reached the driveway at the top of the hill, his car slid in right behind her.

To her surprise, he and Matt and Red got out, three sedan doors opening simultaneously.

She had walked, rather than put Elena in a car seat, and the little girl was starting to feel heavy in her arms. Even so, she paused before moving toward the house.

"Is something wrong?" It was a stupid question. Everything was wrong. But Colby seemed to know what she meant.

"No, everything's going fine down there. Miranda told us you're looking for some muscle. Need to move some furniture around, she said?"

Hayley hesitated. Eyeing the men with wide eyes, Elena lay her head against Hayley's shoulder. The little girl held her ash-covered doll in one arm, and sucked the thumb of her free hand, trying to calm herself. She breathed heavily, choking occasionally, tear tracks trailing down each rounded cheek.

Yes, Hayley could definitely use some help. She'd already been wondering how she'd watch Elena and move boxes at the same time.

But she hated to end up beholden to the Malones. They hardly knew the Eliots. If they did this work, they'd be doing it for her.

"We want to help, Hayley." Once again, Colby seemed to be reading her mind. He smiled. "We're more useful than we look. Back before we got fat and lazy, we cleared out many a warehouse, and furnished many a take-out joint. We're practically the Malone Brothers Moving Company."

A small beige bandage stretched across Colby's left forearm, just below the rolled-up cotton of his long-sleeved shirt. Her chest tightened at the sight. He had been hurt. Not seriously, but Miranda had told her about it when they first arrived. He'd run into the barn to retrieve Elena's favorite doll.

So she already owed him, really. He'd been on the property, getting soil samples, when the fire first started, and he had pitched in to help because…because why? Because of Hayley's connection with this land, and these people?

She shifted Elena in her arms. Wasn't that a little egocentric? Maybe it had nothing to do with her. Maybe he helped because he simply was that kind of person.

An exhausted pressure had begun to build behind her eyes, and she suddenly didn't want to spin around in her own paranoid thoughts anymore. She didn't care whether she ended up owing him. Common sense was stronger than pride.

"Thank you," she said. She dug her key out of her purse and headed toward the front door. "Thank you all. That would be great."

An hour later, though every muscle in her body ached, she knew she'd made the right decision. She couldn't remember the house ever having been so chock-full of noise and bustle. Whatever misgivings she'd had about letting the Malones come to the rescue were banished when she saw how wonderful the brothers were with Elena.

While Colby went upstairs to wash up, Hayley, Matt and Red had stopped in the kitchen, to get water for everyone, and a glass of milk for Elena. As the little girl tried to drink, she began to cry, and finally to talk.

Somewhere in her jumbled, watery words it became clear that what upset her most was the loss of the glittery moon they'd hung just yesterday in the Haunted Vineyard.

Hayley promised her that another moon could be acquired—though, in truth, she wasn't sure how. She stroked Elena's damp, tangled hair, and began softly to sing "By the Light of the Silvery Moon," hoping to distract her.

Without so much as an introduction, Matt walked right over and started singing along. When that song ended, he started up another, this one called "The Man in the Moon." After that, he and Red began singing alternate verses about "The Little Blue Giraffe-Colored Moon," but the lyrics were so ridiculous Hayley suspected they were making it up on the spot.

No matter. It worked. Five minutes later, Elena was giggling, though she still gripped Hayley's shirt with one tight fist.

Soon after, Elena finally succumbed to exhaustion. Matt and Red loped upstairs to help Colby. Hayley followed, and tucked Elena warmly into the sunroom divan—close enough to check on frequently, but quiet and snug enough to let the little girl go on sleeping for a while.

By the time Hayley joined them, the brothers had already designed a game plan. Their task was to clear out one of the bedrooms, and Hayley's was the obvious choice. It was right next to the sunroom, so the Eliot family could spread out a bit.

She wondered if the men would mind moving beds around, after the room was clear. It was a lot to ask, but her father's bed would work better for Eliot and Miranda. Hayley could make do with one of the twins, and then they could put the other twin in the sunroom, and let Elena have her own space.

But oh, the boxes that would have to be relocated! They decided that the quickest fix would be simply to transfer the chaos from her room to Gen's, the one that had been turned into the home gym. The basement was big enough to hold everything, but trekking up and down those stairs, carrying heavy boxes, would have been exhausting—and time-consuming.

She stood in the doorway to her old bedroom, smelling the smoke that had wafted up the hill, and watching the dust motes dance on the stacks of cardboard cubes. Her dad had obviously used whatever he found—and the boxes themselves were a kind of biography. Somewhere along the way, he'd bought a new television, a computer, netting to keep birds away from the grapes, dog food... She paused there. Her dad had owned a dog? He'd never let his daughters even consider such a thing.

And, of course, there was an amazing amount of wholesale liquor. In her day, he'd been a beer-drinker. But at some point, he'd switched to scotch. Ironic, really, that he'd never been able to stand wine.

"It's okay. It only looks intimidating. We'll knock that mountain down in no time." Colby was behind her suddenly, his voice upbeat.

While Hayley and Matt had been calming Elena, Colby had showered in her dad's bathroom and changed into an old jogging outfit he kept in the trunk of his car. He was the only one who had needed to bathe, as he'd done the lion's share of the work at the fire, long before the rest of them arrived.

He still smelled a little smoky, but the effect was nice, like standing near a leaf burn in the woods.

"I should have tackled this sooner," she said, hopelessly. "There wouldn't have been so much to get rid of now."

He laughed and put his hands reassuringly on her shoulders. "The Malone Brothers Moving Company is accustomed to lugging ovens and freezers. A few boxes filled with old shoes and books is child's play to burly men like us."

She turned, smiling. She appreciated his attempt to lighten her mood. "Burly?"

He held up a Popeye-like fist, as if to display his impressive muscles. "You doubt my burliness, madam?"

She chuckled. Oh, she'd forgotten how much she just plain liked him. All three of them. The Malone boys didn't know how to be bored, or depressed or lazy. They had made everything fun. They could take a boring chore, like delivering the last few pizzas of the night, and turn it into a magical ride through space, or a noir private-eye adventure…or merely a carload of nonsense and laughter.

"Never," she said, touching the offered muscle, playing the game. But the minute she felt that familiar contour under her fingers, her throat did a strange tightening thing, and her eyes began to sting.

She let go.

"Thank you," she said. "Thank you for all this work. For caring about Roland and Miranda. For saving Elena's doll…" She swallowed. "For everything."

"It's nothing," he said. He smiled, still encouraging, his eyes locked on hers as if he could infuse her with his good cheer. But then, just as in the vineyard the previous day, the air between them changed. He tilted slightly toward her. His eyes darkened, and a pulse beat in his jaw.

"Really. It's so damn little. God, Hayley… Don't you know that I'd do anything—"

"Hey, slacker! Coming through!" Behind Colby, Red made a beep-beep noise, like a bulldozer thrown into Reverse.

Colby turned, and Hayley could see that Red had found, somewhere, a little red hand truck. She should have thought of that. Even a neglectful vineyard owner had to have some tools.

Time to get to work. They parted self-consciously,

making way for Red. They began piling boxes on the hand truck, and soon they were working like synchronized professionals, all awkwardness forgotten in the backbreaking labor.

But her lips still tingled, from where he hadn't kissed them.

IN THE ORIGINAL DIAMANTE restaurant, which occupied the ground floor of a row of renovated town houses in San Francisco's Lower Pacific Heights, a back room beside the kitchen was always reserved for the Malone family.

Tonight, Nana Lina had gathered the clan together here—and as they waited for Sidney to bring her in, everyone was a little on edge, especially Colby. He had heard a rumor that she'd ducked out on her bridge party early yesterday. Nana Lina didn't play bridge like a socialite. She played bridge like a Green Beret commando. For her to leave early was unprecedented.

Colby had no proof, but his instincts were sending up red flags. He had a sneaking feeling she'd used the extra time to meet with Dr. Douglas. And now a formal family huddle, kids and wives included? He might be wrong about Douglas, but *something* was up.

He had arrived early, and he'd been nursing a glass of zinfandel for half an hour. The wine wasn't very good. This was why Nana Lina wanted Diamante to make its own wine. For years, they'd had trouble finding a unique brand that worked, without pricing so high no one would order it.

Matt and Belle had shown up about five minutes ago, and he had Sarah by the hand. A daddy's girl, that one—and, as the only female born into the family in three generations, guaranteed to be spoiled rotten.

"So…" Matt glanced down at his daughter, obviously aware that little ears were always listening. "You in on the secret?"

Colby shook his head. "I've got a bad feeling, though. Why all the mystery? She's not exactly the cloak-and-dagger type, normally."

Matt shrugged. "Don't borrow trouble. Could be something good. Maybe she wants to announce she's getting married."

"And that would be good?" Colby laughed. "Not for the poor groom, it wouldn't."

But they both knew it wasn't an engagement. Though Nana Lina was glamorous enough to attract any man she wanted, and even dated now and then, she didn't want a new husband. She was still in love with Grandpa Colm. Besides, she always told her three grandsons that she was more likely to murder one of the males she already was plagued with than she was to bring another one into her life.

"Damn, I'm getting old," Matt said, twisting his back as far as good manners would allow in public. He caught his daughter looking up at him somberly, and amended that. "I meant *dang*. Didn't I say *dang?* But honestly, didn't Watson ever throw anything away?"

Colby's jaw felt tight. "Well, he threw his family away."

Matt let that go. Too serious, probably, in front of Sarah, who was too smart for her own good and would undoubtedly repeat every word of this to her mother. Luckily, at the moment she was fascinated by the glimpse of the kitchen, where someone was tossing dough for the next customer's pizza.

"So." Matt seemed to be looking for another subject. "How's the arm?"

Colby glanced down. The bandage was covered by his broadcloth shirt, thank goodness. He didn't want to spend the whole night explaining how he'd tried to play hero at the Eliots' barn fire. He didn't mind the insults Red and Matt had lobbed at him all the way home, but the women were another matter. They wouldn't tease. They'd demand details, burrowing into his emotions like termites.

"It's nothing," he said, exactly as he'd said the other hundred times he'd been asked. "I swear, if I'd known bringing out that kid's doll would lead to all this fuss, I'd have let it burn."

"Sure you would have." Matt grinned. "And have Hayley Watson think you're a loser?"

"Listen, damn it—"

But Colby would have to wait. Nana Lina had finally arrived. She looked great, so pink-cheeked and bright-eyed that for a moment his anxieties were allayed. Couldn't be anything seriously wrong, could there? Not while she stood there looking like Zsa Zsa Gabor.

He went straight to her and kissed her with more energy than usual, just because. She pulled back and gave him a shrewd look. "What? What have you been up to?"

He laughed, taking her arm. "Nothing. We're just starving, that's all. You're late."

Suddenly, he realized it was true. Diamante smelled

heavenly—like sweet basil and honey and warm, crusty dough, pepperoni and sausage and every herb under the sun. Maybe that was why they couldn't find a good enough wine. Nothing could compete with the food.

They placed their orders—although they ate at Diamante so often the kitchen was probably working on Sarah's ham-and-pineapple baby pizza already. And if Nana Lina ever ordered anything other than angel-hair pesto, someone might faint.

All Malone dinner parties were loud and merry, and this one was no exception. But Colby was sure he caught the same undercurrent of anxiety on every adult face he met. Still, eating was no joke for the Malones, so it was understood that, whatever Nana Lina had to say, she wouldn't announce it until after the last uneaten slice was sent to the kitchen to be boxed.

For the entire hour, Colby ping-ponged between worrying about Nana Lina and trying not to think about Hayley. But he couldn't help it. He wondered how the restoration company was doing on the Eliots' house. Probably finished by now—it had been several days.

Roland and Miranda had been embarrassed and had insisted on paying for the work. Though Matt was normally reluctant to be dishonest, he'd assured them that the cleanup team was already on retainer with Diamante, and wouldn't cost a thing.

Hayley had known the truth. Colby had seen the gratitude on her face. And, like an idiot, he ate it up. He really was as big a fool as his brothers thought.

But he couldn't help it. He had this ridiculous feeling, almost a superstition. He imagined that if he could regain Hayley's respect before she headed back to Florida, the rest of his life would finally fall into place.

Like some weird exorcism. He wondered what Nana Lina would think if he told her that.

Finally, after all the wine and colas and pizza and salad, the moment came. Nana Lina waited for a lull in the noise, then spoke.

"Thanks, all, for coming on such short notice," she said. She didn't stand. She didn't need height to command the table. "Especially you, Colby. Now that you have a second job as a firefighter, finding any free time must be very difficult."

The story had made the rounds, of course, so everyone laughed. Including Colby. He was ridiculous. No point denying it.

"However, I've had some news," Nana Lina went on. "And I thought it would be easier if I told everyone at once, instead of going through it a dozen times with each of you separately."

"What kind of news?" Red, who sat to her left, wasn't known for his patience.

"Is it doctor news?" Sarah's booster seat elevated her enough to participate, and she took every opportunity to join the grown-ups' discussions. "'Cause Momma and Daddy said—"

She stared dramatically down at her knee, where Belle was obviously pressing beneath the tablecloth, subtly trying to signal her to hush.

"What?" The little girl frowned, her blue eyes stormy. "You did!"

Nana Lina hadn't been overly sentimental with her grandsons, and she clearly wasn't going to commit that sin with her great-grands, either. She adored them, but she expected a certain level of honor and civility, and simply wouldn't accept anything less.

"Perhaps she did say that, Sarah," Nana Lina said. Though her voice wasn't stern, even an amoeba would recognize that she meant business. "But repeating what you've heard other people say is not always kind. Would you want anyone listening to every word you say and repeating it in public?"

Sarah appeared to think about it. "No. Sometimes I get really mad at Colin."

"Exactly." Having made her point, Nana Lina seemed to be having trouble repressing her smile. Sarah was such a smart little peach, and no one could truly resist her. "Actually, Belle and Matt—and, I suspect, the rest of you, too—have hit on the truth. My news is doctor news."

Sarah lifted her chin and smiled smugly, vindicated. But the adults were quiet. Waiting.

No. Colby said the word over several times in his head. *No. No.*

"Oh, for heaven's sake," Nana Lina said, waving her hand over the table as if she found them all insufferable. "Where on earth did you boys learn to be so melodramatic? Not from me, I hope. I'm going in for surgery, that's all."

That's all? Nana Lina never thought much about her age. She considered it unimportant, just a label other people bothered with. But when it came to general anesthetic, and recovery times, the numbers were real. At eighty, surgery was dangerous. Period.

Finally, the questions came, as if they'd been shot

from scatterguns. The brothers, their wives, everyone wanted to know when, what kind, why, how long, inpatient or outpatient.

Out of the chaos, a picture finally emerged. Apparently she'd sought a second opinion—that must account for the early departure from bridge—and the new doctor had concurred. The atrial fibrillation she'd been dealing with for a couple of years was getting worse, and the medications weren't controlling it. The rapid, irregular heartbeat meant that blood was pooling in the upper part of her heart. Her stroke risk was off the charts, not to mention damage to her other organs, which weren't getting enough blood.

So the docs had settled on something called pulmonary vein ablation. Not open-heart surgery—just catheters, and then some controlled burns to deal with the hinky spots. Nana Lina was downplaying the whole thing, but Matt already had his phone out, looking it up.

"Put that thing away, Matt," she said acerbically. "Do you think I'm in my dotage? Do you think I'm unable to check things out for myself?"

Colby took her hand. "When is it scheduled?"

"A week from Monday," she said. "November fourth. But if you three are going to spend the next week looking like this—"

Red affected an offended air. "Like what?"

"Like basset hounds with dysentery."

Everyone laughed at that, even Sarah, who seemed to think *dysentery* was a hilarious word. She said it about six times, until Belle leaned down, smiling, and commanded her to stop.

Colby met Matt's gaze across the table, and reluctantly, Matt put the phone away. Colby caught Red's eye, too, and Red nodded. They understood. This was only Saturday, just the twenty-sixth of October. So that gave them a whole week—no, eight days, to check into all of it. The surgery, the risks, the doctor himself.

If some sawbones thought he was going to mess with Nana Lina's heart, he was going to have to go through all three of the Malone brothers first.

CHAPTER TEN

THE MINUTE HAYLEY stepped inside the front hall of The Sonoma Academy the next Monday afternoon, she had to fight to keep her head above a flood of memories. This private K–12 school was the only one she had ever attended—until the night they left California for good. After that, since Hayley had only her senior year to complete, she'd worked through her GED instead of attending class. So any happy school memories all lived here, in this graceful, two-story white building surrounded by palms.

Ordinarily, Ben Watson wouldn't for a moment have considered springing to send his daughters to a private school. But Evelyn Watson had worked as the school nurse, and one of the perks was reduced tuition.

Elena, who walked between Hayley and Miranda as they entered the building, squeezed Hayley's hand tightly—and probably Miranda's, too. She hadn't been truly relaxed since the barn fire.

When she was extremely nervous, she communicated mostly in nonverbal ways, and she clearly was intimidated by the shadowy halls—hushed now, as classes were over for the day—that loomed in every direction.

Hayley smiled down at the little girl. "It's really big, isn't it? I remember the first day I came here. I was so scared. But once I got used to it, I loved it. It was like a second home to me."

Or a first home, she thought. Here, order reigned. Here, everyone wanted to see her succeed, and believed she could.

Here, even her mother had been a completely different person. All the students loved "Nurse Evie," from the queasy kindergartener who'd eaten the delicious-looking periwinkle crayons, to the coolest senior softball star who had taken one on the chin.

But Elena's grip didn't relax.

"She's right," Miranda echoed. "The students here are very nice. Just wait till you see the pretty new moon they've made us!"

Elena blinked up at her grandmother, then at Hayley, liquid eyes searching. Where there should be the easy, smiling trust of a four-year-old, Hayley still saw doubt. Elena didn't automatically believe anything grown-ups told her. She was waiting for proof.

Hayley's heart squeezed. So many ways you could mess up as a parent. She said a quick prayer that, when her turn came, she wouldn't make any whoppers.

One thing she knew, without question. Once the warm, tiny hand she held belonged to her own child, she wouldn't be letting go. Ever.

"Here we are," Miranda said enthusiastically as they entered the auditorium, probably to negate the eerie hollowness of the large space. All those rows of empty chairs and the mysterious blue velvet curtain that undulated in the air coming from the vents. "I think they're around behind the stage."

Students from the Academy's drama club had played

the Silver Moon Fairy at the Haunted Vineyard ever since Hayley's time, so of course they'd heard about the fire that had damaged several of the event's props. The older kids, the juniors and seniors, probably knew the Eliots well, as they always worked the event alongside students from schools all over the area.

Still, it had been a happy surprise when Mrs. Mignon, who still ran the club even after all these years, had called Miranda this morning. The students had built a new moon, she said. If Miranda could pick it up, they'd be in the prop room behind the auditorium anytime after four.

When Hayley heard, she'd asked if she could come along. She hadn't ever belonged to the drama crowd, but Mrs. Mignon also ran the Latin club and taught English, both of which Hayley had loved. Seeing the tough old lady again would be a special treat.

Even hearing that Colby would be coming with Roland to load the moon into the truck didn't change her mind. Colby and Roland were meeting this afternoon to discuss the possibility of adding some of Roland's grapes to make Diamante wine. She wasn't feeling quite as prickly toward him now, not since he'd been such a champ during the fire's exhausting aftermath.

As long as they didn't spend much time alone, she should be fine.

The minute they rounded the corner, Hayley heard the buzz of teenage voices. They opened the door to the back room, and suddenly the atmosphere changed completely. In here, a dozen students milled about, some in frilly, bewigged costumes, some bent over colorful set designs, pounding hammers or sprinkling glitter. In one corner, three girls performed a dance without music. In another, a pair of boys lunged at each other, thrusting rubber swords, but laughing so hard they could hardly remain erect.

As she gaped at the vibrant scene in front of her, Elena's hand went slack in Hayley's. She seemed too surprised to remember to be afraid.

"Hayley!" A tall, regal woman, the one adult in the room, hurried over, arms outstretched. "Great Caesar's ghost, I thought I would never lay eyes on this child again!"

"Mrs. Mignon," Hayley said. And then, without warning, she found herself wet-eyed and fiery-throated.

She accepted her favorite teacher's embrace, even as she registered how frail the woman had become. Mrs. Mignon's hair had always been salted with white, but she'd kept it long and wound it up into a glorious head-dress worthy of Calpurnia. Now it was so short and thin and gray that Hayley suddenly knew the truth. Mrs. Mignon had been very, very sick.

When the older woman drew back, she had tears in her eyes, as well. She didn't brush them away— she had always been comfortable with emotion. One of the qualities that made her such a wonderful teacher and actress. "Ah," she said with satisfaction as she scanned Hayley from head to toe. "Radiant. 'Herein lives wisdom, beauty and increase.'"

Hayley laughed in a sudden deep delight. Mrs. Mignon had always offered a Shakespeare quote for every circumstance. Her students had pretended to groan, but they'd secretly loved it. Shakespeare's words made all their trivial events and temporary passions sound so profound.

Hayley still remembered the time Mrs. Mignon had found her crying in the girls' bathroom, at the end of junior year. She had just heard that Colby might not be working at Diamante that summer. The Shakespeare quote Mrs. Mignon had offered that day had been oddly prophetic.

"Strive for balance, Hayley," she'd said, her gray eyes pensive. "Remember, 'these violent delights have violent ends.'"

If only Mrs. Mignon had known how violent.

"Thank you," Hayley said now, putting the past aside and acknowledging the compliment. "But radiant? I wish that were true. Maybe I just look happy to see you." She glanced at the cheerful, humming room. "I can't believe it's been such a long time! Everything looks almost exactly the same. What are you performing?"

The older woman's eyes twinkled. "*The Importance of Being Hamlet,*" she said with a grin. "You'll have to see it to believe it. December second. I'll send you all tickets!"

Hayley bit her lip. She'd be back in Florida long before that. Should she say so? But Mrs. Mignon had already turned to greet Miranda and Elena, and was leading them over to the workbench in the center of the room.

A few of the students clearly had been given the task of presenting the creation when they arrived, and were excited about their mission. As Elena approached, two boys and a lovely brunette girl rushed to the bench and lifted up a huge, elaborate construction.

The kids had outdone themselves—the moon was bigger and more impressive than ever before. It was essentially a black wooden bench swing with a crescent moon attached to it by ropes. The ropes had been painted black to make them disappear into the October night sky, leaving behind the illusion of a moon suspended in space.

Even in here, in the day, the moon itself was the only thing anyone noticed. At least three inches thick and six feet high, it sparkled under the overhead light as if it burned with some kind of fire made of diamonds and pearls. It must have been sprayed an inch thick with iridescent glitter—and the effect was magical.

Elena gasped. She put out one hand, as if in a trance. Then she glanced up at her grandmother, suddenly remembering that she probably should ask permission to touch.

Miranda nodded. One of the boys lifted Elena so that she could reach the entire moon, and to Hayley's surprise, the little girl didn't resist the unfamiliar hands. She touched her trembling pink fingertip to the lower point of the moon, and made a soft sound of delighted wonder.

"Hayley, look," she breathed.

Hayley smiled. "I know. Isn't it wonderful?"

The brunette girl touched Elena's curls, smiling. "I am friends with the Silver Moon Fairy, Elena. And she told me she wants you to be her assistant this year. Would you like to do that?"

The wide gray eyes said it all, but Elena nodded emphatically anyway, and kept nodding, as if she weren't even aware of doing so.

The Silver Moon Fairy had been the centerpiece of every Haunted Vineyard Hayley could remember, and apparently nothing had changed. The fairy sat on the crescent moon swing, holding a sparkling silver fishing rod. As each child came to make a wish, she lowered the rod into a cauldron and "caught" a present. It was never anything expensive, mostly candy and trinkets, but it was the perfect activity for the children who were too young to enjoy being scared by the tombstones among the grapevines or the skeletons in the barn. No one went away disappointed.

They'd have to pick a different tree this year, and move most of the decorations out into the open, now that the barn was gone, but somehow they'd make it work.

Mrs. Mignon came up beside Hayley, and put her hand through Hayley's arm. "She's precious," she said. "How about you? Are you married? Do you have a family?"

"Not yet." Hayley refused to sound wistful. She smiled. "Someday, though."

"Yes. Someday *soon,* I hope." The older woman squeezed Hayley's arm. "I've thought about you so often. I kept hoping perhaps you would come home."

"I missed you, too," Hayley said honestly. "But coming back to California simply wasn't possible."

"Wasn't possible until *now,*" Mrs. Mignon amended. "Finding your way back takes time. 'What wound did ever heal but by degrees?'"

Ah, Shakespeare again. And, as always, the teacher

was right—the bard knew the human heart better than anyone.

"Mrs. Mignon, I'm not staying," Hayley said abruptly. She hadn't meant to blurt it out like that, but she suddenly felt as if she were swimming against a strong current that would, if she let it, suck her back into her old life. "I'm here only to sell the vineyard and arrange my father's affairs. My life is in Florida now."

"You say that very emphatically," the teacher observed. "Is the emphasis for my sake, or your own?"

Hayley sighed. "Mine," she admitted. "Shakespeare is right. Wounds have to heal by degrees. Though it took a long time, mine almost had healed. Until I came back here."

Mrs. Mignon frowned. "I thought perhaps, with your father gone…"

"It's not just my dad." Hayley tried to think of a way to put it. She wished she had some convenient Shakespearean quote to explain things for her. "Old memories…they have a way of opening things up again. I need to leave, so that I can get back to healing."

At that moment, Roland and Colby came through the door, shoulder to shoulder, laughing and jingling the truck keys, as comfortable as old friends. Their meeting must have gone well.

Though, to Hayley's knowledge, Mrs. Mignon hadn't ever met Colby officially, she probably recognized him. Ridley was a small town, and when personalities as potent as Colby and Matt Malone spent even the summer there, they got noticed. Girls became flustered and extra girly. The boys grew territorial and tried to compete. You might as well put a shark in your living-room fish tank.

"Ah, yes. Old memories," Mrs. Mignon said thoughtfully, as she watched him compliment the kids on the silver moon. "'But men are men. The best sometimes forget.'"

Hayley glanced at the older woman. That was a quote she didn't know, and couldn't interpret—not while her mind was disrupted by the sight of Colby coming toward her.

Her reaction to his undeniable sex appeal no longer shocked her. She'd hoped that such things died, particularly when starved for years on end. But now she knew they didn't ever really go away. A chemistry existed between the two of them, and it was no more their choice than it was the choice of sugar to dissolve when plunked into water.

How she responded, though, *was* her choice. And she chose to respond with maturity and self-control.

She smiled as he came closer. "Hi," she said, as if the air between them wasn't as filled with opalescent sparks as that Silver Moon over on the workbench. "Colby, have you ever met Mrs. Mignon? She was my English and Latin teacher when I went to school here. She's the advisor for the drama club, too. Mrs. Mignon, this is Colby Malone."

He held out a hand, his charisma shimmering like a halo all around him. "Mrs. Mignon, it's a pleasure to meet you. The moon is fantastic."

"Thank you," Mrs. Mignon said, taking his hand and holding it an extra second, almost as if she were analyzing his pulse, or his nerve endings, like some mind reader at a carnival. In her thin, gray face, her eyes were sharp and inquisitive. "I've certainly heard a lot about you, through the years."

The cliché answer to that, naturally, was something like "All of it good, I hope?" But Colby didn't fall into that trap. He obviously knew the answer to that question was likely to be a resounding negative.

"And I have heard much about you," he countered with a smile. "In fact, I've heard that you have a Shakespeare quote for every person, and every occasion."

Stupidly, Hayley blushed. She didn't recall telling him that, and she was stunned that he'd remember it.

Mrs. Mignon looked neither surprised nor flattered. She returned his smile with an equable nod. "Yes, that's true. I do. In fact, I have one for you, perfect for this occasion."

One of his eyebrows went up in a sardonic arch. Unless he had changed a lot, that trick meant he was uncomfortable, off guard…and hiding it. "Is that so?"

"Yes. That's so. Do you want to know what it is?"

"Of course I do," he said chivalrously. "I have to admit, I'm flattered. Surprised, but flattered."

"Don't be," Mrs. Mignon said calmly. "As Hayley told you, I have a stockpile. If you'd brought your brothers, or even your dog, with you today, I would undoubtedly have one for them, too."

Colby laughed, not at all offended to have been put in his place. "Understood," he said humbly. "But I'd still like to hear it."

She cleared her throat, as she often did when she was about to recite. "All right. I suspect you can find your way around a poem, if you have the right incentive, so I won't insult you by interpreting. It's a simple one, anyhow."

She glanced briefly at Hayley, then back at Colby's smiling face. "'Better three hours too soon,'" she said, "'than a minute too late.'"

CHAPTER ELEVEN

COLBY WASN'T EXACTLY sure how he'd convinced Hayley to ride home with him in the truck, with the silver moon tethered to the flatbed with bungee cords, as if they'd been out hunting magical creatures and bagged a big one. He'd used a combination of complicated logistics about letting the Eliots ride together in Miranda's car, and some phony-baloney about having some questions concerning the grape contracts.

And maybe he got a little bit lucky. Maybe she was still feeling benign toward him because of the fire. It felt a little scuzzy to exploit that—he certainly hadn't helped the Eliots because he expected it to buy him credit with Hayley. But if it made her feel less antagonistic toward him, he was grateful.

He glanced over at her now. It had taken a while to load the unwieldy moon into the truck, so it was nearing sundown. The air was chilly, but she had her window open. She'd always liked the fresh air. In high school, he'd had a vintage black Mustang convertible he'd bought with his own money and planned someday to restore. Hayley had loved the banged-up little car, too. Sometimes she had stood in her seat, hands in the air, laughing at the feel of wind rushing through her hair.

Today, the dying light was yellow-orange, and their

path pointed them due west. He had to wear sunglasses, but even so, he could see that the glow lit her whole face and caught on the feathery tendrils that had escaped her braid. It created a halo effect around her elegant profile, which was a little intimidating.

How did you ask a saint out on a date—even a platonic one?

"Hungry?" He put his gaze back on the road, as if the question were inconsequential. "We could grab something quick on the way home."

She took a deep breath, rubbing her fingertips across her temple as if she were tired. He wondered how hard she'd been working, trying to get through all her father's debris in record time. Maybe her employers were stingy with personal leave time. She acted as if there were a time clock counting every second until she could get back to Florida.

And the baby she planned to adopt.

"Actually, I'm starving," she said, surprising him. He'd assumed she'd say no, she had too much work to do at the house.

"Yeah?"

"Yeah. I haven't eaten since…sometime yesterday. I finally tackled the financial records early this morning, and I worked straight through lunch. Any kind of fast-food would be great."

He smiled. "I know a terrific pizza place."

She yawned, apparently too tired to protest. "If they still make that fabulous Hawaiian pizza, I could definitely go for a slice of that."

"You and Sarah." He laughed. "So predictable."

She didn't respond, and suddenly he wondered

whether she thought he was referring to another girl-friend.

"Sarah is Matt's little girl. She's three, and she could eat our Hawaiian pizza all day, breakfast, lunch and dinner."

"Smart kid," she said softly. He glanced over again, and saw that she'd let her head fall back against the padded headrest, and her eyes were shut.

He removed his sunglasses, then took out his phone to place the order. When he did, he realized he'd missed several calls. He must have forgotten to take the phone off vibrate when he got out of this morning's meetings. He hoped none of the calls had been about Nana Lina.

He scrolled through the list. Nothing from the family. In fact, most of the calls had been from Marguerite. She'd left three voice messages, which he wasn't about to listen to now, with Hayley only eighteen inches away. Marguerite's voice had a penetrating quality, especially if she was upset, and three voice messages certainly suggested she was.

Some warning instinct throbbed dully inside him. When you dated as many women as he had over the past seventeen years, you were bound to run into a few who didn't have all their bolts tightened down. But Marguerite hadn't struck him as one of the flakes. She was a nice woman, and a smart one.

Which is why this felt wrong. And a little troubling. If she was hounding him, she probably had a pretty good reason.

Even so, tomorrow would have to be soon enough to deal with whatever it was. Tonight…tonight he had Hayley Watson in his car again, with the sunset in her hair and a rare absence of tension in her body. He was going to savor the moment, if he could.

The kid who answered the phone was sharp enough to know who Colby was without being told. He seemed to get the order right the first time, and promised it would be ready in ten minutes. Colby got the boy's name and made a mental note to give him a raise. Alert, focused teenagers were hard to hire and even harder to keep.

In fact, he thought, remembering how obnoxious he and Matt had been back when they answered the phones, this kid was nothing short of a treasure.

After he picked up the pizza and a couple of cans of Coke, he climbed back in the truck, tucking the drinks into the console holders, and handing the pizza box off to Hayley. She inhaled appreciatively and murmured something wordless, then let her head drop back onto the headrest.

He knew he ought to take her home. She was tired. She probably wanted to throw on an old T-shirt, eat her pizza in bed and fall asleep watching something mindless on TV.

But he was selfish, and he wanted more time.

When he got to the turnoff to the Foggy Valley drive, he idled the car. Up ahead, just a block or two beyond her road, was the wooded overlook, a thick stand of redberry, plum and pear trees at the crest of a hill, which gave way to a spectacular view of a bowl-shaped vineyard valley below. Depending on the time and weather, the bowl could be filled with sparkling sunlight, or swirling fog or creamy moonbeams, but it was always a sight of breathtaking beauty.

So many nights, when they had been reluctant to say goodbye, they'd driven out there and sat in his car, listening to the wind in the treetops, talking about nothing.

Okay, so most of the time they'd done a lot more than talk. Especially on nights when the fog rolled in, so dense no one could even see his black Mustang, much less what was happening inside.

"How about if we eat this at the overlook?" He glanced at her. She had her eyes open, but the sunset was almost gone, and the last inch of sky had dimmed to an oxblood red. Reading her expression was almost impossible. "Roland and Miranda were going to stop for dinner, so they won't be ready to help unload yet."

She hesitated. She shifted the pizza box pointlessly, clearly buying time to think.

"It's a nice night," he said. He nodded toward the flatbed. "And even if it weren't, we bring our own moonlight."

She smiled. "No fog?"

He almost laughed out loud. She remembered. Of course she remembered. It was just that, sometimes, their romance seemed so long ago it felt like a book he'd read, instead of something that really had happened. It felt like an old legend, a myth, a ghost story about the laughing girl with sunshine hair who blew away on a cold midnight wind.

"I can't make any promises about the fog," he said, choosing his words carefully. Maybe he was overanalyzing it, but she seemed to be asking him whether he intended to use the overlook the same way he always had—as a place to get his hands on her irresistible body. If that's what she meant, he didn't intend to start out with a lie. "I'm not really in complete control of the weather."

Her eyes glimmered in the dusk light. "Of course you are," she said, eliminating all doubt about whether this conversation had subtext.

He did laugh out loud this time. She had always delighted him with her candor. Most of the girls he'd dated had been masters of flirtation and coquettish conversation, but Hayley had liked to be honest and real.

"Fair enough," he said. "So…how about this? If you're uncomfortable with the weather…or with anything, we'll leave."

She nodded slowly. "Fair enough," she echoed, though she sounded unconvinced, and some of the tension had returned to her body. Her fingers were braided tightly together on top of the box.

When he parked at the overlook, she grew even stiffer, and an awkward silence filled the truck. He shook his head, internally. She looked as nervous as a hitchhiker who had foolishly accepted a ride from a weirdo.

What did she think he was going to do? Had he ever so much as touched the back of her hand if she said no? He'd dated her three summers running before she even let him unbutton her shirt. At sixteen, seventeen, eighteen, he hadn't been very patient with overly good girls who blushed and giggled and said yes, then no, then yes, then no. He'd preferred openly lusty, fun-loving girls who kept their feet on the gas.

Every summer, he told himself he wouldn't call Hayley again when he got to Ridley. But every summer he did. He called, he kissed, he controlled himself. He played by her rules, without even understanding why.

And then he found out why. That last summer, in a flood of unleashed passion, she'd suddenly succumbed. And the experience had turned him inside out. His groin tightened now, just remembering the shock of sex with Hayley. She'd made the other girls look like shadows.

"Come on," he said, grabbing the drinks from their holders. Maybe if they weren't locked in this small cab together… "Let's get some fresh air."

She followed, clearly relieved, balancing the pizza box as she climbed down from the high perch and found the ground. He plucked a blanket from under the glistening moon, and they walked to the nearest stand of redberry trees. They were high enough, far enough from Foggy Valley, that they could no longer smell the charred wood from the fire.

Overhead, stars had started to appear in the blackening sky. They blinked on, one at a time, as if in some distant world unseen creatures were lighting lamps against their own darkness.

He'd always loved this view, especially on a clear night. Moonlight streamed across the acres of Ellenton-Barnes pinot vines. EB Valley was the oldest vineyard in the area, designed long before automation was even possible. It had narrow rows, and every so often a real tree had been left standing to provide havens of shade for tired vineyard workers.

He opened the blanket, and they sat—not so near that their arms actually touched, but close enough that he could feel her warmth radiating out from beneath her soft blue turtleneck sweater. She smelled of roses.

He shut his eyes briefly. It was a new perfume—not the scent she used to wear. But beneath the roses, there was only Hayley. And that was piercingly the same.

For a few minutes, they merely ate, letting the wind sweeping the treetops be all the sound they needed. By the time Hayley finished her first piece of pizza, she seemed more relaxed. With a low sigh, she tilted her head back and stretched her neck. Her long braid swayed gently against her shoulder blades.

"It was strange going back to the Academy," she said out of nowhere. "Mrs. Mignon doesn't look well. In fact, she looks terrible."

"Does she?" He hadn't known the woman before so he had no point of comparison. "What…you think she's sick?"

"Yes. Or has been."

He could tell she was upset at the prospect. "Maybe. She looks pretty tough, though. If she's battling something, I'd put my money on her."

"Yes." She let her gaze fall pensively on the land below them, which was dreamlike tonight, pearly gray in the moonlight. "Still, it's weird, thinking that all these things have happened while I was gone, and I had no idea."

He smiled. "I know what you mean. It would have been nice if Ridley could have stood still, like a village trapped under a snow globe."

"No, it's not that I believed…" She shrugged. "I guess I thought it didn't matter, because I wasn't connected to Ridley anymore. I thought I wasn't even the same person. But I guess I am. Whether it makes sense or not, I still…care about some of my old friends."

His fingers twitched on the blanket. "Of course you do."

"I don't know…" She had a strip of crust in her hands, and she rotated it absently, like some kind of worry stone that helped her think. "I didn't expect this. I thought people would mostly have forgotten us, or moved away themselves. It's been so long."

Forget them? He wondered if she realized what a legend the missing Watson women had become locally. Because Diamante had several locations near here, he and his brothers still spent a good deal of time in the area, and they heard things. Especially the things they were interested in. His attention always sharpened when someone mentioned the rumors about the Watson women.

The rumors probably would have died long ago, if they hadn't been so tragically romantic. Would it embarrass her to know that boys would sometimes sneak their girlfriends into Foggy Valley at night and tell them the story of the mysterious baby who cried when the moon was full, or the ghostly girl in white, searching the vineyard for the infant she could never find?

The baby was made up, just for melodrama. Ironic, really, how the gossips had managed to get some of the details right without even realizing it.

When Ben Watson caught the teens, he usually chased them off with a BB gun. Fleeing from an old drunk, dancing around the BBs that kicked up dirt near their feet, wasn't a macho look and definitely put a crimp in the boys' seduction plans.

Colby decided not to say anything. He didn't want to interrupt this contemplative mood, probably brought on by the visit to her old school. She seemed much less guarded now, and he wanted to hear everything he could.

"I guess I thought it would all seem more remote," she went on, still twirling her bit of crust. "But people have been so... They bring casseroles, and they call and they stop me in stores. The Eliots, Mrs. Mignon, Mrs. Blythe. And I saw Merry Evans the other day. I even ran into Tim Bern, and he—"

She stopped, and finally she turned to look at him. Her face was somber in the pearly moonlight. "Ridiculous, isn't it? Seventeen years...literally half my lifetime. And yet I still feel awkward saying Tim's name in your presence."

"You don't need to," he said softly. "I realized long ago how wrong I was about all that."

She nodded. But she still looked sad, and slightly confused, as if she couldn't make sense of her own emotions. Tim Bern had been her first boyfriend, a good-looking, studious boy who had clearly loved her. A boy who had been willing to wait until her madness with Colby Malone wore off.

He'd waited almost three years. The eldest son of a big, well-respected Sonoma family, Tim had been there at the end of that last summer, when Colby and Hayley had fought over his impending departure for college. Tim had comforted her, taken her to the movies, held her hand and promised her she'd get over Colby eventually.

And, in that innocent offer of support, Tim had unwittingly provided Colby with the excuse he needed. Colby had been able to pretend that he thought honest Tim Bern could be the real father of Hayley's baby. He told himself that it was a short trip from comfort to seduction…and he should know, having clocked the mileage himself more than once.

He wished he could go back and shake some sense into his young self. But he couldn't. All he could do was admit what he'd done without trying to justify it.

"Did you believe it? I mean…really believe it?"

What was the answer to that question? Yes? No? Yes and no? He'd asked himself a million times, and never found anything that felt like certainty.

At the time, he'd desperately wanted to believe it. He'd been panicked at the thought of losing his freedom. Embarrassed that he, of all boys, had been foolish enough to get "caught." He'd worked so hard at blaming Hayley that it was almost impossible to know what his real feelings had been, under that avalanche of fear and shame.

"No," he said, surprising himself with how absolute the answer was when it came out. "No, I didn't believe it for a single second."

He knew this admission only compounded his sin—after all, fingering Tim as a potential lover, too, must have, from her father's uptight perspective anyhow, made her look little better than a slut. But he couldn't help it. He'd always known that Hayley hadn't slept with anyone but him. In her absence, everything about that time had seemed jumbled and confused. Now, in her presence, it was all suddenly as clear as the sky overhead.

For a minute, she didn't respond. Then finally she smiled, just a little. "Good."

For the first time in seventeen years, a knot inside his chest relaxed. For a few minutes after that, they sat quietly, enjoying a silence that seemed somehow cleaner, the way the air can be washed fresh by a summer rain.

"Mrs. Ellenton-Barnes is interested in buying Foggy Valley, too," she said, when the silence had stretched as far as it could go. She didn't look at him, letting her gaze fall pensively on the land below them, where wisps of fog had crept in and were licking the trunks of the vines. "Did Greta tell you that?"

"She told me I wasn't the only one," he said. "She didn't give me details. But I'm not surprised. Foggy Valley used to have a real name around here. There will be others, once the word gets out. And that's okay. All I ask is that you give me a chance to counteroffer."

She turned. "Why?"

Somehow, in the past few minutes, they'd inched closer on the blanket, and when she turned their faces were so close he could see the tiny, white line that ran across the bridge of her nose. She got that scar one night when they were running through the trees, eager to get their clothes off and their hands on each other's bare skin. In his haste, he'd let a tiny branch whip back and slash her across the nose like a razor.

He reached up and ran his thumb along the mark. "I remember when this happened," he said, ignoring her question. She didn't flinch or pull away, so he let his thumb stroke it again, lightly. "I was always hurting you, wasn't I?"

She had begun to breathe shallowly. He felt the warm, light exhales against the inside of his wrist.

"Not always," she said.

The two words were spoken softly. They sounded… almost…like forgiveness.

He moved his hand to her cheek, then to her ear and finally slid it to the back of her neck. He tunneled his fingers into her hair, working through the barrier of the braid to cup the fragile roundness of her head.

He tried to wait, to see if her neck stiffened, praying she wouldn't pull away. Desire dug its claws into him, and he had to fight to keep his touch gentle. He wanted… Damn, how fiercely he wanted to pull her into his arms and kiss her until the regret of the past and the question mark of the future both disappeared into the fire of right now.

He searched her face for a sign, and found it. Her eyes…they gleamed in the moonlight, shining with need.

"Hayley," he whispered. And then, his nerve endings firing in painful anticipation, he lowered his lips to hers and reclaimed what once was his.

Her lips were hot and sweet, and they parted almost instantly, as they always had, welcoming him into the even hotter darkness of her mouth. He groaned, and took it all. His other hand went around her waist and pulled her body into his, breast to chest, beating heart to beating heart.

She held back maybe three seconds, and then he felt her yield and sink into him. Her hands rose and threaded themselves into his hair.

Hayley…

He struggled to hold himself in check. Her touch was so familiar, so knowing and perfect that he could hardly stop from climaxing right there like a high school kid, just because he also knew how those fingers would feel on the rest of his body.

And yet…this wasn't like being eighteen again. It was far, far worse than that. He couldn't ever remember, at any age, feeling so completely at the mercy of a woman. He didn't just want her. He needed her. Without her, the pain that had been eating at him for seventeen years would come back, and he would go screaming, raving mad.

He kissed her until their lips were swollen and wet, and their hands were hot from roaming hard and hungry against the clothes that stood between them.

And then, like a fool, he pushed it too far and broke the spell. Without thinking, he pressed her, urging her down toward the blanket. Everything in him operated on autopilot. His body knew what it needed, and wasn't in the mood to stop and think. But instantly he felt her spine stiffen. Her lips cooled, and their pliant edges tightened.

She tilted her head back, creating a tiny fraction of space between them. "Colby."

He stopped pressing her toward the blanket, but he couldn't make himself let go. "I'm sorry," he said. He was breathing heavily, and he rested his forehead against hers, trying to gather his wits. "I know it's… it's too fast. I…I wasn't thinking."

Beautifully put, Romeo. How could she resist him now? Panting and stuttering were such a turn-on.

Where were all the smooth lines he'd used with a hundred females?

Gone. Just gone. All that slick romancy charade… gone. Probably never to return. "Hayley, I'm sorry. I'll go slowly. I won't…"

He clenched his jaw. Why couldn't he think of the right words?

"It's all right," she said calmly. "I'm sorry, too. But, in a way, we probably needed to do that… Obviously we both wanted to know how it would feel." She smiled. "But now we really should be getting back."

For a minute, he couldn't believe this was her voice he heard. After that kiss—such a small word for what they'd shared—shouldn't there be emotion, struggle, passion, awe?

Shouldn't she sound…changed?

Did she really think they'd just tested out this kiss, the way they might taste a new flavor of cola to see if it was any good?

"Colby," she said again, when he didn't answer. "We need to get back to Foggy Valley."

And then, while he was trying to find the magic words to make her stay, she wriggled away from him, tugging her sweater into place. His hands went limp.

And, whether he could bear it or not, it was over, and his chance was gone. There were rules, even for men who had just stepped off the cliff edge and no longer had solid ground beneath their feet. He had to let her go.

CHAPTER TWELVE

FLORIDA. BRILLIANT AND blistering. Palm trees waving against a white, sun-washed sky, like an overexposed picture postcard from long, long ago.

Hayley was home. And yet, somehow…it didn't feel right.

She stood in the front window of the little College Park house she and Genevieve had rented for the past ten years. They'd taken it right after their mother's death. It had felt momentous, signing that lease, using their real names for the first time in so long.

She could hardly believe how different everything looked, after only two weeks away.

Even at the end of October, the grass was thirsty brown beneath the shockingly vivid spiky red ixora hedges. Stray dogs languished in any shade they could find, and the bees on the honeysuckle seemed drugged with sun.

Was this really home? As the cabdriver had pulled onto her street, she'd had a momentary panic that she wouldn't be able to tell which of the little pastel-painted cinder-block houses was hers.

In the end, naturally, she had recognized it. But she still felt oddly out of place. She'd dressed too warmly, and by the time she'd made the short walk from the driveway to the front door, she had been simultaneously sweaty and baked, the nape of her neck damp, but the skin on her face drawn tight, like bacon in the pan.

Now, an hour later, having changed into something more tropical, she stood holding on to her elbows and waiting for the phone to ring. She reminded herself that this dislocated feeling was probably just nerves. The news that had brought her home was disturbing, and it was affecting her reactions to everything.

Joyce Tichner had called in the wee hours of the morning. She'd apologized for phoning so late. She couldn't have known that Hayley had been wide-awake for two nights straight, tossing and turning and trying to forget the feel of Colby's lips.

Joyce told Hayley that her daughter, Anna, was in the E.R. She'd begun spotting, and with the pregnancy only six months along, the doctors didn't want to take any chances. They'd monitor her overnight, at least.

Nothing really frightening—Joyce had been calling only to let Hayley know. Partly as a courtesy, since Hayley paid all medical bills associated with the pregnancy. And partly as a friend who knew how important the baby was to her. Mother to mother-to-be, so to speak.

Joyce undoubtedly hadn't imagined that Hayley would take the first flight out of California, zigzagging the Midwest in the middle of the night so that she could be there. Just in case.

Not that there was anything she could do. Anna had the best care central Florida had to offer, and after that, the outcome was in the hands of Fate. Anna wouldn't even want Hayley in the hospital with her, hovering. She had her own mother, and Hayley would be in the way, maybe even an uncomfortable presence, like the landlord standing over you at payday, making sure you didn't squander the rent.

Still. Impossible to remain a continent away while her ba— She stopped herself. Not her baby yet. While *Anna's* baby was in any kind of danger.

All the way here, Hayley had rationalized the decision. She could accomplish other things while she was in town. She missed Gen, and it would do her good to spend at least a few hours with her sister. And she really should talk to her bosses, face-to-face, and explain exactly how much more time she was going to need in California.

Plus, she simply needed to breathe air that wasn't filled with the presence of Colby Malone.

That kiss they'd shared on the overlook had shaken her to the core. The kiss, and all the intimate things that would have followed after, if she hadn't somehow stopped herself. She had ached all night, as if her body mourned the emptiness left behind.

She glanced over at a picture of her mother, which Gen had painted in college and had hung on the wall ever since. Gen was a dancer, not an artist, so it wasn't particularly good, except that she'd gotten the eyes exactly right. Blue, beautiful. Sad, but filled with love.

She could almost hear her mother warning her. *If you give him your heart, Hayley, he'll break it. He might not mean to, but he will.*

No. Standing here now, she promised her mother she wouldn't let that happen. No matter what it took, she had to be smarter than that. When she left Sonoma for good this time, she was not going to be hauling a big fat broken heart in her baggage.

Never again.

From the side yard, over in the driveway shared by this house and the identical one next door, she heard a car door slam. It might be Mrs. McGill, their landlady who lived in the other house and owned them both. Hayley listened, hoping the elderly woman wouldn't come over to chat. But then she heard the light skip of footsteps. Not Mrs. McGill, who had arthritis and poor balance.

It must be Genevieve. Suddenly the little living room seemed less oppressive. Gen had that effect everywhere she went.

Her sister came in, humming, sharply dressed in a navy blue suit, her arms full of packages and mail. She paused just inside the doorway, looking up as she sensed that she wasn't alone.

"Hales!" Squealing, Gen dropped everything at her feet, then dashed over to wrap Hayley in a warm hug. No matter how old Gen got, or how expensive her cosmetics and perfume now were, Hayley would always smell baby shampoo and talcum when she embraced her little sister. She hugged back, hard, drinking in the uncomplicated love.

Perhaps Gen felt something out of proportion in her sister's clasp, or maybe she just put the pieces together. Whatever the reason, she pulled back suddenly with a frown between her round blue eyes.

"What are you doing here? I thought you'd be in Sonoma for another week, at least." She bit her lower lip. "Something's wrong, isn't it?"

"No." Hayley shook her head reassuringly. She kept her voice calm, instinct taking over—the instinct to protect Gen from all unpleasantness.

But she also never lied to her sister. "Well, nothing serious, anyhow. It's just that—I heard from Joyce last night. Anna is in Orlando Regional because she began spotting a little bit yesterday. They're just being super-careful, but I thought maybe I should…"

Ugh. She thought maybe she should *what?* Fly across the country just so that she could do her fretting in the same city as the pregnant girl? So that she could wave her please-please-don't-lose-the-baby wand over Anna's hospital bed?

The decision sounded even dumber when she said it out loud.

Thankfully, Gen wasn't the type to tease her about it. "Of course you had to come home," she said, as supportive as ever, but clearly worried. "I know! Want to go over to the hospital now and check on her? Give me a sec to change out of this iron-maiden suit, and I'll come with you."

"No. I think I'll wait a bit. I don't want to pester them."

Hayley glanced again at the nook of the bay window, where an armchair and a small table were placed, facing in toward the sofa. Her cell phone was the only thing on the table—except for lamps and coasters, it was the only thing on any surface in the room. The Watson women didn't go in for clutter. They didn't buy knick-knacks and souvenirs everywhere they went, like some people.

Guests often complimented them on how peaceful

and stylishly streamlined their home was. They didn't realize that it wasn't a design choice. It was merely that, having jettisoned a lifetime of precious sentimental pieces once, they had no heart to start another collection now.

The phone lay there, small and silent. Hayley repressed a feeling of impotent frustration. Why didn't Joyce call? She'd promised to keep Hayley updated, and it had been twelve hours now since she'd heard anything. She tried not to think that was a bad sign. Maybe Anna had already been discharged, and in the commotion of settling back in at home, they'd let that detail slip.

"Okay." Genevieve still looked concerned, but she didn't argue. "Well, later, then. We'll go over later."

She went back to pick up the packages and papers she'd dropped. As she arranged the shopping bags on the dining-room table, Hayley suddenly caught a glimpse of something sparkling under the overhead light.

"Gen?" She moved closer to get a better look at her sister's hand. "Gen! Is that what I think it is?"

"Huh?" Genevieve frowned, but then awareness seemed to dawn. "Oh." Oddly, she looked almost guilty, and instinctively put her hand down. "Oh, darn it! I didn't want you to find out like this!"

"Genny, show me!" Hayley reached for her sister's hand and dragged it back out into the light. On the ring finger of her left hand, Gen wore a brand-new, absolutely beautiful diamond solitaire. A big one—obviously expensive. It winked and sizzled, throwing off prisms of color. "Oh, my God. Tommy asked you—and you said yes!"

"I'm sorry I didn't tell you…I wanted to wait until you got home…" Gen tried to hold back her excitement, but after a few seconds it just wasn't possible. She reached out and hugged Hayley all over again. "Can you believe it, Hales? I'm so unbelievably happy. I feel like dancing all the time."

Hayley laughed. Genevieve always felt like dancing. Her irrepressible spirit was infectious. It was like living with a rainbow. Hayley liked Tommy Davis a lot, but she hoped he realized how lucky he was.

Genevieve did a joyous pirouette, then settled in the glow of the dining-room chandelier. She grinned, wiggled her ring to catch more light, and broke out laughing, as if joy were a bubbling spring inside her. "Isn't it gorgeous? I've been dying to email you a picture, but Tommy said we should wait until we were all together. I think he's worried—"

She broke off, a cloud passing over her face. "I mean…we're both worried…"

"About me?"

"Well…"

"Gen, no." Hayley could imagine where this was going, and she needed to nip it in the bud immediately. She drew her sister over to the sofa and pulled her down so that they sat knee to knee, and eye to eye.

"Worried about me?" she repeated insistently.

Genevieve nodded. "I hate to leave you alone—and especially after the baby comes, I know you'll need help. If we could stay here, it wouldn't be so bad. But Tommy is up for a promotion—and if he gets it, he'll have to move to Phoenix." A small line formed between her brows. "Phoenix seems so horribly far away."

Hayley took her sister's hands—both of them. "Gen, listen to me. I want to say something really important. I don't want you to argue with me. I just want you to listen, and try to really hear what I'm saying."

Genevieve met her gaze somberly. "Okay."

"I want you to know that, if you are in love with Tommy Davis, and he's in love with you, you mustn't let anything stand in your way. Not *anything,* do you understand?"

Genevieve nodded again. "Yes. But I love you, too, and—"

"And I'll be fine. That's the truth, pure and simple. If you're happy, I'll be more than fine. I'll be ecstatic."

"But—"

"No arguing. Just hear me. Will I miss you? Of course. But your happiness means everything to me. Can you imagine how happy Mom would be? It's been a long time since we…left California. And through it all, one of the hardest parts for both of us was knowing how much you lost, all because of me."

Gen started to protest, but Hayley stopped her with a gentle jostle of fingers. "If, in spite of everything, you've found your happy ending, don't you see how wonderful that is? Don't you see how it finally makes everything right?"

Her sister's eyes were shining, but she swallowed hard and managed a smile. "I guess so," she said tremulously. "Although can't you see, Hales, that I wish the same thing for you, and—"

The cell phone rang, abnormally loud in the small

room. Without a word, their hands squeezed tightly, and their gazes held.

It had to be Joyce. It had to.

When it rang a second time, Hayley unfroze. She stood, let go of Genevieve's comforting grip and forced herself to walk calmly to the little table. She picked up the phone and answered it.

Genevieve might have been a statue, sitting immobile on the sofa, her unblinking eyes trained on her older sister. Her thoughts were silent, but their intensity reverberated invisibly in the currents of the room.

The caller ID confirmed it was Joyce.

"Hello?" Hayley glanced toward the picture of her mother for luck, then held her breath until she heard Joyce speak.

"Hayley, I just wanted to tell you she's home."

Joyce's voice was filled with emotion. But what emotion? Grief or relief?

"She's feeling great," Joyce continued. "The doctors said she should take it easy, but they're sure everything is going to be fine."

And then the air burning in Hayley's lungs all came out at once, in something that sounded like a cross between a whoosh and a cry. Alarmed, Genevieve half rose, her arm outstretched, but Hayley shook her head, smiling.

She put her hand over the speaker. "She's okay," she said. Her voice broke, but she said it again. "She's okay."

And suddenly, there in the sparely decorated, tiny living room, under the watchful eyes of their mother's picture, both Hayley and Genevieve were crying tears of relief and joy.

Once, it hadn't seemed possible. But finally, after all these years, after the running and the fear and the loneliness and the loss, they both had a chance to find that miraculous happy ending.

THE NEXT DAY WAS HALLOWEEN, and Hayley had booked an early flight, so that she'd be back in Sonoma in time to help with the Haunted Vineyard.

After Genevieve and Tommy drove her to the airport, kissed her goodbye and waved until the tram took her too far away to see, Hayley sat in the boarding area, waiting for her nonstop flight back to San Francisco.

The plane would be crowded. Even here in the rows of the waiting area, she was squeezed in between two businessmen who were making constant calls on their cell phones, as if the world couldn't keep turning without their direct involvement in every rotation.

Which reminded her, in some illogical way, of Greg....

As the attendant came over the loud speaker, announcing boarding of the first few rows, Hayley pulled out her own phone and put in a call to Greg's practice. It was Thursday, so he should be in the office. Halloween wasn't the kind of holiday that obstetricians took off.

"Hi," she said when Deirdre, the scheduling manager, answered. On the spur of the moment, she decided not to identify herself. "I wondered...would it be possible for Dr. Valmont to work me in today?"

"I'm sorry," Deirdre said. "Dr. Valmont is on vacation this week. Dr. Kensington is filling in. Would you like an appointment with him?"

"No," Hayley said, a frisson of discomfort running through her veins. "No. I'll wait for Dr. Valmont to come back."

She glanced up as the businessman to her right stood, gathering his briefcase and striding with poise toward the gate, still talking loudly. It hadn't ever occurred to him that he might be annoying anyone. He didn't think in those terms.

Just like Greg.

Well, two could play that game. Hayley laughed artificially, putting as much snooty elitism into her voice as she could, hoping Deirdre would assume she was one of Greg's more important patients.

"Lucky Dr. V." That's what the rich, flirtatious ladies liked to call him. "He's always going somewhere wonderful. Paris last summer, as I recall." She laughed intimately. "Where is he this time?"

Deirdre laughed, too. "Not Paris this time. But almost that nice. He's out in wine country. I think he said Sonoma."

CHAPTER THIRTEEN

LUCKILY, THE PLANE wasn't late, so Hayley was back in plenty of time to help the Eliots set up for the Haunted Vineyard. While she was in Florida, the little family had moved back into their own home, and she knew that her house would be sadly quiet tonight.

So for the time being, she was glad to be part of the bustle and happy hubbub of the Halloween party.

The weather was going to be perfect for it. She could smell the clean, cool evening approaching. The charred boards of the barn had all been trucked away, so the only burning smell was a sweet, smoky hint of someone's leaf fire in the background. The sunset had begun early, as if the sky were eager to put on its Halloween costume, too—a ragged witch's skirt of purple, bloodred and black.

For hours, Elena had been beside herself with excitement. The event wouldn't begin for another hour, but she was already dressed in her costume—a white sequined fairy tutu, complete with glittery wings, clearly chosen because it would look perfect next to the silver moon.

The little girl was supposed to be helping set out candy to put in the prize bags, but she kept eating every third piece. Finally Miranda, who could see a sugar rush coming, followed by the inevitable sugar crash and tears, sent the little girl off to help Hayley lay out the pumpkin-bowling lanes.

The "lanes" were really just rows of vines, marked off by neon orange sand. The kids would roll actual pumpkins as far as they could, trying to knock over some discarded old bowling pins painted to look like witches.

The lanes couldn't be set until the last minute, because they were so easily destroyed by rain or wind or careless feet. Hayley poured the sand from a bag as she moved slowly down the row, and the task was too strenuous for a four-year-old to be of much assistance. In fact, Hayley's back was already aching from bending over at this awkward angle so long.

She had this one last lane to finish, and a little white fairy fretting around her feet, begging for an assignment. So she created the job of line-checker, which meant that, whenever any of the orange sand went astray, Elena had to push it back into place with a stick.

"Peepaw hanged the moon," Elena told her as they worked. "Did you see it?"

"Yes," Hayley said. "It's beautiful."

And it was. Even in the sunset, every time it shifted even a fraction of an inch, a thousand sparks flashed. By moonlight, it would be eerie and mysterious.

"He won't let me ride it," Elena said sulkily.

Hayley glanced up, surprised at the fussy tone. Usually Elena was a quiet but uncomplaining child. "Well, he has to be sure nothing bad happens to it before the party."

"I wouldn't make anything bad happen," Elena said. She kicked at a messy part of the orange line, but in her temper she kicked too hard. Dirt flew all over the line Hayley had put down, as well as all over her pretty white satin ballet slippers.

Guiltily, she looked at Hayley from under lowered brows. "Sorry," she mumbled, then bent down and tried to brush the dirt away. Her efforts just made things worse, but Hayley decided to deal with it later. She wondered what was wrong with Elena.

"I hope we have time to take a nap before the party," she said with a smile as she reached the end of the lane. "I'm so tired from my airplane ride. Are you tired, too?"

"No." Elena put her thumb in her mouth, a habit she resorted to only when she was deeply upset by something. "I'm not a baby. Babies take naps."

Hayley laughed. She put the bag of sand down and straightened, so that she could rub the small of her back. "Then I must be a baby, because I'm going to take one." She brushed her hands together. "Come on. If you don't want to take a nap with me, I'd better walk you back to your meemaw."

She half expected the little girl to change her mind. During the few days the Eliots lived in Hayley's house, Elena and Hayley had become great friends. Instead, she walked quietly beside Hayley as they went back down the hill to where Miranda was working.

"There's not time for a nap anyhow," Elena said, her tone still sullen.

Hayley pushed back the black wool of her sweater and glanced at her watch. "You're right," she said evenly. "Let's just see if your meemaw needs help, then."

Down by the house, Miranda was putting on the finishing touches. Everything had been moved outside, because of the barn fire, which meant none of it could be done until they were sure it wouldn't rain today.

Almost ready. But with only half an hour to go, Haley knew they should expect early strays to start showing up any minute.

"Let me help," Hayley said, grabbing one of the large bowls filled with the steaming neon-green liquid they called Putrid Punch, and setting it on the table Miranda had just draped with a purple tablecloth. She stepped back and admired the effect. "Fabulous. Very creepy."

"Thanks," Miranda said, but she didn't take long to enjoy her success. She began setting out the bags of candy, each tied with a frilly orange ribbon. Hayley grabbed the second carton of bags and began doing the same.

"Did it go okay in Florida?" Miranda's glance at Hayley was maternal, full of unexpressed uneasiness. Hayley had told her about the baby last night—she'd had to. Otherwise, her strange flight in the middle of the night would have been just too alarming.

"Everything is fantastic," Hayley said, sorry that she hadn't found a moment to put Miranda's mind at ease sooner. She'd arrived only two hours ago, and by then everyone was crazy busy. "Anna is well and healthy. My boss seemed very understanding about my taking a little more time, and Gen is officially engaged."

She grinned. "It's like the trifecta of excellent news."

At that, Elena plopped onto the ground, apparently not caring if her lovely spangled costume got filthy.

"You want to go away and live there." She glared at Hayley accusingly. "With your new baby."

Ahh…so that was the cause of all the petulance. Hayley and Miranda exchanged a quick look. Miranda shrugged, as if to say it couldn't be helped, but Hayley's conscience stung. Maybe she shouldn't have been so guarded. She should have mentioned the baby right from the start, so that this wouldn't have come as a shock to the child.

But she hadn't imagined that little Elena would become attached to her so quickly.

She considered sugarcoating it somehow, but that was the coward's way out. Elena was right. Hayley would be leaving in a few days, and she probably would come back rarely, if at all.

She squatted in front of the child, smiling but serious. "Yes, I am going to have to go back to Florida, because my house and my family are there. But I will miss you and your meemaw and peepaw very much. I hope you'll write me all the time and tell me what's going on at school, and in the vineyards."

Elena tugged at the strap of her ballet shoe for a minute, pouting. Then finally she looked up at Hayley. Her face was contracted in a scowl so intense it almost looked comical.

"Well, I won't," she said furiously. "I don't like Florida, and I don't like babies."

Hayley nodded. Right now, Elena reminded her very much of Genevieve, whose sunny nature had sometimes darkened with a storm like this. It always came from fear. "I understand. That's okay. I'll write you, instead."

Then she stood, aware that she couldn't do much

more right now. Luckily, in a four-year-old's life, two weeks was little more than a blink of an eye. The truth was, Elena would forget Hayley long before Hayley forgot the little girl.

Miranda seemed to sense that a distraction was in order. "Come on," she said. "Peepaw wants you to test the swing now."

And, as if to prove Hayley's theory, Elena jumped to her feet, crying out joyously, her snit forgotten. She raced ahead of her grandmother, impatient to climb onto the magical moon and fly into the sky.

Inexplicably, as Hayley watched the little white twinkling figure disappear, her heart ached. How, she wondered, had this trip home become so complicated?

Colby, of course. But not *only* Colby.

She scanned the rolling hills of the vineyard, mellow and soft-edged under the deep twilight-blue of the sky. For one effervescent, fleeting instant, she felt fifteen again, and had to fight the urge to start running, laughing, chasing her friends up and down the rows of vines, filling her lungs with the cold October air.

The vineyard looked and felt exactly the same, as if she'd stepped into a time machine, and stepped out again, twenty years in the past. She'd seen it all before…the little fake-granite tombstones, the swinging white-sheet ghosts, the fairy lights twinkling among the leaves and the Silver Moon swaying and sparkling in the rising breeze. The changing colors in the forest, and the loamy scent of earth and growing things. The black silhouettes of birds beating the sky, and the last of the fall crickets humming in the woods.

How could she have forgotten how much she loved this land?

It didn't matter that these acres now belonged to Roland. It didn't even matter that for every happy memory she had of this place, there were two sad ones. Somehow, deep down below the workings of her heart and brain, this was the world that her soul understood.

"Hey, there." Colby appeared beside her suddenly, as if her imagination had conjured him, one more ghost arriving to join the ghosts of the long-vanished laughing friends and the fifteen-year-old Hayley who chased them through the vines.

She turned, feeling her cheeks grow pale. She would have known, if she'd thought about it, that he would come tonight. He'd called, several times, while she was in Florida, but she hadn't answered. Worrying about Anna, and the dangers to the pregnancy, had been all the stress she could handle.

She also hadn't been ready to take on the task of figuring out what to do about that kiss.

But now that he was here, she knew there was nothing to figure out. She already knew what she had to do.

He was smiling, his profile strong and unfairly handsome against the endless blue twilight, which, she realized suddenly, was exactly the color of his eyes. The moon had just appeared in the western sky, and its soft beams made his black, wavy hair look like rippled velvet.

He was dressed all in black, as she was—the default "costume" of the adult too busy to bother with masks and claws and devil ears. Or perhaps the name of that costume was Temptation. Memory. Regret.

"Colby," she began.

"I've brought some people I'd like you to meet," he said. "Sarah? Colin?"

He motioned to a pair of children who were pressed against the refreshment table, watching the punch with openmouthed wonder. Roland had hidden dry ice beneath the greenery around the punch bowl, and poured a dozen green glow-in-the-dark ice cubes into the lime-ade, so the effect was pretty spectacular.

The children turned reluctantly. They'd dressed as pirates, both of them, and they already wore the glow-stick necklaces and bracelets that were handed out at the front gate. Miranda had added that touch, so that no child could end up lost, wandering at midnight in the maze of vines.

"Come meet Hayley," Colby said. The children, who were probably about Elena's age, trotted up obediently, grinning and elbowing each other in goofy high spirits. "Hayley, this is Captain Sarah."

The little girl scowled.

Colby laughed. "Excuse me, that should have been Captain *Jack Sparrow* Sarah." He grinned at Hayley. "She's Matt's little girl. And this is Sir Colin Black-beard, her hapless prisoner. He's David Gerard's son. A good friend of the family."

He nudged them forward. "Guys, this is Hayley Watson. She's an old friend of mine."

"Hi," the kids said in unison, which made them giggle and bump each other some more.

"Hey," Hayley said. The little boy had a smart, en-gaging, Huckleberry Finn face, and a riot of uncontrol-lable blond curls. The girl had the unmistakable Malone coloring—dramatic blue and black over porcelain skin and pink cheeks. She would be a beauty someday. "Nice to meet you, Captain Sarah and Sir Colin. I hope you have a wonderful time at the party."

She turned to Colby. "Is there any chance we could talk for a—"

But to her dismay, she couldn't even finish the sentence. Apparently the influx of Malones had only just begun. Behind the children trooped a crowd of adults—Matt and Red, each of them holding a baby in one arm and a lovely young woman on the other. And there was another man, too, some kind of blond Adonis who was obviously little Colin's dad. The woman who walked beside him wasn't a beauty, but she seemed to glow with an inner fire that made beauty irrelevant.

And behind them all came Angelina Malone and an elderly white-haired man who had the dignity of an ambassador, though he wore only blue jeans and a plaid flannel shirt.

The exchange of pleasantries and introductions seemed to take forever. Hayley had once imagined the Malones as a snooty, exclusive clan that would treat any outsider like an interloper. But she'd been wrong. They were noisy and fun, relaxed and unpretentious. Even the wives and fiancées were extraordinarily friendly and welcoming.

They all had a glow of physical vigor and a certain athletic fitness, as only people with lots of time to play outdoors and lots of healthy food to eat could achieve. But other than that, you'd never know they were anything but one more happy family enjoying the Haunted Vineyard with their kids.

Even Angelina seemed completely unintimidating tonight. She greeted Hayley warmly, and introduced her to her companion as a "dear family friend." In spite of his ordinary-guy clothes, and his whimsical chain-link lei of glow-in-the-dark circlets, Hayley wasn't surprised to discover that the old guy's name was famous in California political circles.

Eventually, though, the kids lobbied hard to explore the vineyard, and everyone finally wandered off. Hayley had to go help at the pumpkin bowling game, but she managed to touch Colby's sleeve just as he was about to walk away.

"Is there any chance I can talk to you just a second? Alone?"

Colby smiled. "I can try. But maybe later would be better. Maybe dinner, tomorrow? Privacy is pretty hard to come by in this crowd."

"No." The last thing in the world she wanted was another dinner with him. "I mean—it won't take long."

His expression sobered. "Okay."

"I just wanted to say...I mean, I just wanted to be sure—"

Hell. She'd rehearsed this in her head a hundred times. On the plane coming back, she'd sorted out what she should say, so that there would be no hard feelings.

He didn't interrupt her. He just waited, his eyes picking up the starry twinkling from the Silver Moon.

"It's about the other night. When we..."

He smiled slightly. "Kissed."

"Yes. When we kissed. I want to say that I know it wasn't your fault. Deep inside, I knew that might happen, if we went to the overlook. It was inevitable, really. We should have known better."

He tilted his head, making the glints in his eyes wink disconcertingly. "Should we?"

"Yes. You know we've always found it difficult to be…wise…about things like that. I thought it might have changed. We're so much older now."

"Ancient," he said, still smiling that mirthless smile. "But apparently no wiser."

"No." She put her hand up to her temple, which had started to throb. "Well, maybe a little wiser. At least we didn't let it go so far that…we didn't take any real risks."

He nodded slowly. "Is that something you don't do anymore, Hayley? You don't take risks?"

She flushed, but she stood her ground. "Not that kind of risk."

"What kind is that?"

The kind that has already almost killed me once, she started to say. *The kind that could take this new life I'm trying to build in Florida and smother it under an avalanche of heartbreak, before it even has a chance to grow.*

But that was too melodramatic. Remember how she'd hoped to end this civilly, so that both of them could move forward lighter, happier, free of the past? Why was sanity so difficult for her, where this one man was concerned?

Sarah came running up to her uncle, her plastic sword bumping her knee with every step she took. "Uncle Colby, Mom says I can't go in the fortune-teller's tent unless I have a grown-up, and Daddy won't go. Will you take me? Please?"

She grabbed his hand and tried to pull, but Colby didn't take his eyes from Hayley. "What kind of risk is that?" he repeated.

"Risk means there's a *chance* of losing, a *chance* of getting hurt," she said. "I go back to Florida in a week, Colby. So, with you and me it's not a *chance* of losing. It's a certainty."

His adorable, impatient niece was practically dangling from his arm, trying to budge him, but he didn't move an inch. He might as well have been an oak, from whose branch she swung, leaving his roots undisturbed.

He still kept his flashing eyes trained on Hayley. "And if I disagree?"

"Please. Don't." Hayley rubbed her arms, suddenly cold as the night wind gusted. "Take Sarah to the fortune-teller's tent, Colby. The psychic will tell you the same thing. If you and I were to get involved, even for one night, it wouldn't be a risk. It would be complete and utter madness."

CHAPTER FOURTEEN

"You okay, Uncle Colby?"

Sarah's blue eyes were droopy and tired, but still uncomfortably observant as Colby carried her to her dad's car a couple of hours later. She was wearing his windbreaker, because her pirate costume had proved too flimsy for the cold breeze that swept across the vineyard as the night wore on.

"I'm fine, Captain," he said with a smile. Nana Lina would accuse him of being a chauvinist, but dang. Was mind reading a gift females magically received in the womb? Belle and Kitty and Allison had been asking him the same question all night long, though he was quite sure he wasn't acting strange in any way.

And he wasn't all that upset, anyhow. Sure, Hayley's words had sounded final. In fact, they'd sounded about as final as a slammed door followed by the clinking of a tossed key.

But her body language...

Her body language said something else altogether. Her eyes had been dark, sleepless, haunted. She'd stood back, as if she were afraid to get too close to him.

And she had hummed like a live electrical wire, the kind his dad had taught him to watch out for after a storm. Some downed wires just lay there, dead as dead could be. But others had a different feel, a trill of danger silently coursing through them, even though they might not look a bit different on the outside.

Bottom line—Hayley still thrummed when she was around him. She wasn't dead. She wanted to be, maybe. But she wasn't.

And there lay all the difference in the world. There lay hope.

Nana Lina had left after only about half an hour, at her grandsons' insistence. Her surgery was next Monday, just a few days away, and though they couldn't hold her prisoner, they didn't intend to let her take any chances. So that left David, Red and Matt, and their families. Sarah and Colin, little pistols that they were, could have held out another hour, but the babies were fussy and crying, which meant the ladies were ready to leave.

Okay by Colby. He intended to hang around a while, and the sooner the rest of the gang went home the better.

Miranda, who seemed mutely sympathetic to his cause, put him to work at the refreshment table for a while, but by ten, demand for Putrid Punch had tapered off, and she clearly didn't need him anymore. He decided to walk around a little. A gang of rowdy teenagers had showed up a while back, and he wanted to make sure they weren't terrorizing the younger kids.

He'd attended the Haunted Vineyard event half-a-dozen times, more or less, over the years. He'd come as a teen, with Hayley. And then he'd come as an uncle, with Sarah and Colin. But this year, for the first time, he felt hyperaware of how many strangers the festivity brought onto the private property—and how impossible it would be to make sure that all of them had safely departed at the end of the night.

He understood why he had this new perspective. It was the idea of Hayley sleeping alone in that big house on the hill, surrounded by acres of nothing but vineyards bathed in shadowy moonlight.

He left the main area. He might not be a teenager anymore, but he hadn't forgotten that the prime mischief-making spots were over where the trees formed a rim of privacy for...whatever. Not that he was keen on causing trouble for some poor kid just trying to get lucky. But if he busted up something stupid...well, so be it.

He'd learned the hard way that sometimes *not* getting lucky might be a hell of a lot safer in the long run.

The moonlight coming over the treetops threw shaggy shadows, long and thin and black, onto the vineyard. He'd just reached the ragged edge of the first shadow when he heard a sound he didn't like. He paused, listening, separating this sound out from the partygoers calling and laughing just a few dozen yards away.

It didn't sound like someone getting lucky—even someone young and awkward and imitating the noises they'd heard in the movies. It sounded unhappy, like an abandoned kitten, or a baby.

Good thing he didn't believe in the vineyard ghosts. He could imagine how, if you were an imaginative seventeen-year-old, a sound like this could make your arm hairs stand on end.

When he was fairly sure which direction the sound came from, he moved quietly into the trees. The muffled whimpering came and went, but by now he was sure it really was human crying. A very small human.

The sound grew louder and then, just as he passed under an oak with low-hanging branches, it stopped.

The fall leaves were crunchy underfoot, so he knew the weeper in the tree must have heard him coming. He decided to announce himself, just in case the arrival of a tall male stranger dressed in black came across as menacing.

"Hi," he said conversationally. "Everything okay up there?"

The tree shimmered slightly, more a movement of the shadows on the ground than the branches themselves. He heard a sound like a loud sniff. And then, finally, an angry little voice.

"No."

He smiled at the forthright simplicity. Little kids were just great, weren't they? They didn't think it was weird to be mad as hell, even if their predicament was their own fault.

He peered up into the branches, and saw a little blob of moonlight perched on a thick branch about ten feet up. The blob moved, and he recognized those sparkles caught in a fluffy skirt of net and tulle. Elena.

Damnation. Did Roland and Miranda even know she was gone? She was way, way too high for a four-year-old. He'd have to be careful not to say anything upsetting. The last thing he wanted was to send her skittering higher…or startle her into losing her balance.

"No?" He walked around the base of the tree, trying to evaluate the best approach. "How come? What's the matter?"

"I'm mad," Elena said matter-of-factly. "And I'm stuck."

"Oh." He adopted exactly the same unemotional tone. "Want some help?"

A momentary hesitation. "Are you Hayley's friend Colby?"

He stood still and turned his face up, smiling. "Yep. And you're Elena, right?"

"Yeah. You look different from up here."

His smile deepened. "And you look different from down here."

She sniffed again. Her nose was probably running from all that crying, and he hoped she wasn't letting go of the tree branch to wipe it.

"I came up here because of the man," she said, her voice suddenly plaintive instead of angry.

His blood chilled a degree or two. "What man?"

"The one who was watching Hayley. I didn't want him to see me, so I came up here. But when he went away, I couldn't get down."

Colby considered his options. He could go get Roland and a nice big ladder. But to do that, he'd have to leave Elena alone here.

Whether there really had been a man "watching Hayley" or not, Colby wasn't leaving. No way.

"Is it okay if I come up, too?" He hadn't ever been more grateful that Matt and David had given him some experience with little kids. He at least had a hope of getting the tone right. "I bet I can help you get down."

"I can't," she said. He was glad to hear she sounded more fussy than freaked out. "I tried, but it's too scary."

He had already caught hold of the first branch and

hoisted himself up onto it. It was strong enough to hold him, so he stood and tested the next branch up. Elena was only about three feet away now. She'd put her head down on the branch, so that she was actually stretched out and straddling it. She looked a little like the Cheshire cat, all big, blinking eyes while she calmly watched him climb.

"Hold on tight," he said, and quickly closed the distance between them. The bark was rough under his palms, but the ancient tree was huge, and thank God he didn't have to worry about the branches accepting the weight of both of them.

When he reached the branch just below her perch, he could stand there and meet her gaze. He was relieved to see that, when she sat up straight, her back pressed flat against the fat old trunk.

"Hi," he said, as if he'd come up purely for the pleasure of chatting.

"Hi," she answered. She had both hands on the branch, as if she were riding a pony bareback. She was merely six inches away. She couldn't fall now, unless she fell to the other side, away from him.

Once he'd imagined that, though, he had to fight the urge to reach out and grab her. But would a stranger's hands clutching at her be too terrifying? Right now she was stable. If he tried to pull her down, but didn't get hold of her on the first try…

She stared at him thoughtfully a moment, then peered back down at the ground. When she lifted her gaze to him again, she looked disgusted. "Now we're both stuck."

"Naw." He smiled. He held up his cell phone. "Now we call your peepaw and tell him to bring us a great big ladder."

As it turned out, Hayley had thought Elena was with Roland. Miranda had thought Elena was with Roland.

But when his cell phone rang, Roland was in the house. Asleep. At least an hour before that, he'd gone inside to change out of his work boots, which were giving him blisters. He'd sat down on the bed, just for a minute, while Elena waited in the living room.

When she discovered him asleep—dead asleep even though he'd promised to finally take her out and let her help the Silver Moon Fairy dispense gifts—Elena had decided the injustice of grown-ups was just too much to stand. She'd walked out the back door. She took a bag of candy so that she never had to come back. She'd show everyone just how mean they'd been.

It broke Hayley's heart to see how hard Roland took it. By the time Elena was safely on the ground again, the older man was practically in an agony of self-recrimination. He couldn't stop asking himself...what if something terrible had happened?

But it hadn't. Thank God, it hadn't.

Her pretty fairy costume was mangled and stained with tree sap and mud. Her hair was matted, and her face was streaked with tears. But she was all in one piece, and safe in her own room.

And once again, Hayley had Colby to thank.

Now, they sat in the Eliots' small living room. Hayley stared anywhere but at Colby. She looked at the wicker basket of Elena's toys, imagining how heart-breaking the little pile of stuffed bunnies, crayons and colorful board books would be if tragedy had struck out there tonight.

If Colby had not been making sure all was well.

They clearly both were trying not to hear Miranda's stern tone, or Roland's anguished pleas, as the two tried to impress upon the little girl just what a terrible risk she'd taken. But it was a small house, and sound carried.

Finally, Hayley's eyes met Colby's, and they both smiled uncomfortably. She'd already thanked him, and he'd brushed it off. She didn't know what else to say. After the conversation they'd had earlier about the kiss, any further chitchat felt awkward—and besides, everyone was bone-tired and emotionally wrung out.

Eventually, he stood. She stood, too. The teenagers from the Academy drama club had closed down the Haunted Vineyard for the night, so everything was quiet outside. At least she could walk him to his car.

When they got to the porch, though, he paused. She was moving ahead, but he put out his hand and grabbed the tips of her fingers to stop her.

"Wait," he said. "I need to talk to you about something."

Her fingertips tingled where he had hold of them. The tingle ran up her arm and ended in a cascade of gooseflesh across her shoulders. She was too tired for this, she thought. Too tired to keep up the wall that protected her from him.

If he tried to kiss her right now, she would probably let him.

But he didn't look as if he had seduction on his mind. In fact, now that she studied his face carefully, she could see that his features were uncharacteristically serious.

"What is it?" She glanced inside, realizing that he'd

deliberately waited until they were out of earshot to bring this up. Was it something about Elena? Had something else happened out there in the woods? "Colby, what is it?"

For a minute, he looked past her, toward the vineyard. He scanned the middle distance, a landscape mottled with moonlight and shadows. Finally, he returned his gaze to her.

"I don't want to scare you," he said, still holding her hand. "But Elena said something odd tonight, and I think you ought to know. She said she saw a man out there, in the woods. She said the man was watching you."

Now the goose bumps were multiplying, racing down her chest and up into her hair. There was nothing sexy about them. She let go of his hand and leaned against the front porch railing for support. "Who?"

"She didn't say. I got the impression she didn't know him. She just called him 'a man.'" He stepped closer, near enough to look carefully at her face. "She may have been making it up. You know how children are. The line between reality and imagination is pretty fluid."

"Did she say what he looked like?"

Colby shook his head. "No. No details at all." He frowned. "Why? Is there someone you think it might have been?"

She hesitated. She hadn't wanted to mention Greg to Colby. She wasn't sure why. Maybe she was just embarrassed that she'd picked such a terrible boyfriend. Or maybe she didn't want him to know that she had no one waiting for her at home.

But this changed things. This went beyond silly pride.

"There is someone," she said slowly, sticking to the basic details, just as she had with Greta Kinyon the other day. "His name is Greg. Dr. Greg Valmont. I dated him for about a year. We broke up maybe two weeks before I came out here. He…he didn't take it very well."

Colby's shoulders stiffened. "Did he hurt you?"

"No. No. Nothing like that. It's just that he seems to think I might change my mind. When I left Florida, I didn't tell him where I was going. I figured we were finished, and it wasn't any of his business. But he tracked me down, and he flew out here. He just showed up at the house one day last week and seemed to think I'd be delighted."

Colby looked almost angry. "Damn it, Hayley. The guy is a freak. Why didn't you tell me?"

She lifted her chin. "Why should I tell you? I'm not in a relationship with you, either, Colby. Neither of you has any right to be told what I'm thinking, or doing. I can take care of myself."

"And what if it was Greg tonight? Out there in the woods? Watching you?" Colby's voice was flat, but hard and unrelenting. "What if he's still out there now?"

"He's not." She wished she sounded more confident. "Greg's just arrogant and spoiled, not dangerous. Even if he was out there earlier, by now he's in a five-star hotel, ordering room service and checking his messages. He's a doctor, Colby, not a maniac."

He wasn't convinced. She recognized that stubborn set to his already square jaw. He was trying to keep from coming across as overbearing, but it was obviously a struggle.

"Hayley, be reasonable. You need to take this guy seriously."

"And do what? Are you going to move in? Are you going to guard me, day and night, from guys who want to 'watch' me? Where does it end? Are you coming back to Florida with me, so that you can move in there, too? Can Diamante do without you for the next…oh, ten years or so, till Greg gets obsessed with someone else?"

"Don't be ridiculous." He scowled. "I'm just asking you to be careful. Let's call the police, just get it on record. We'll check him out, find out whether he is, as you say, at a hotel. And just for tonight, I could stay at your place." He held up a hand. "On the sofa."

"No." She tried to picture sleeping at all, knowing he was downstairs….

"Then, stay with the Eliots. They have a sofa, too." He ran his hand through his hair. "Or go to a hotel. Just for tonight."

Suddenly, she was simply too tired to argue. And the truth was, these shivers wouldn't stop chasing each other up and down her spine, back and forth across her collarbone. Every time a shadow moved in the vineyard, or a bird squawked in the treetops, another shiver broke out and joined the race.

She hated to give in, but in the end she knew Colby was right. Tonight, for her, this vineyard really was haunted. Her imagination already regularly supplied her father's ghost pacing the inside of the house. Now it would add Greg's shadowy presence, obsessively pacing the perimeter.

"All right," she said wearily. "You win. Tomorrow, I'll call the police. Tonight, I'll go to a hotel. Alone."

HE LEFT HER AT THE HOTEL, though it was all he could do not to follow her up to the room, knock on the door and beg her to let him in.

He pulled the car out of the hotel parking lot and pointed it toward San Francisco. Its bustling density seemed a million miles away from this quiet, rolling rural landscape. If only he could snap his fingers and make the forty minutes between here and there disappear.

It was going to rain again, after several days of beautiful weather. Well, at least it had held off long enough for the Eliots to hold their Haunted Vineyard. The barn fire had been challenge enough. They didn't need another soaking to spoil their time-honored tradition.

He turned on the wipers, streaking away the foggy condensation that obscured the windshield. He rubbed his eyes, too, wishing he could do the same thing with his internal fog.

God, he was tired. Maybe it was just as well Hayley had said a firm good-night in the lobby. He didn't have the energy to be much use to anyone tonight—in bed or out.

And yet, when his cell phone rang, his heart flipped excitedly in his chest, thinking that maybe she'd changed her mind. At least she might be in the mood to talk for a while. She used to like that…whispering into the phone for hours, waiting to fall asleep.

He was so sure it was Hayley that he answered it without even looking, something he almost never did.

"Hi," he said softly.

"God, Colby, I can't believe you answered. I must have phoned you a million times. You sure have been doing a good job of avoiding me."

It wasn't Hayley. It was Marguerite. He thumped the heel of his hand against the steering wheel, and switched the phone roughly to his other ear.

"Marguerite." He forced a polite tone through clenched teeth. "Sorry. I've been really busy. How've you been?"

"Not good," she said. Her voice was strangely tight. What was that all about? Hard to believe she was merely upset that he hadn't returned her calls. They hadn't dated in almost two months, and she had no reason to expect him to jump just because she whistled.

"No?" He steered his car up onto the freeway entrance, following the taillights in front of him. "I'm sorry to hear that."

"Sorrier than you know," she said, her ordinarily mellow, sexy voice thin with tension. She tried to laugh, but it wasn't very successful. In fact, it was downright disturbing.

"What's wrong, Marguerite?"

"Damn it, Colby. That's what I've been trying to tell you. I think—" She choked on the next words and had to try again. "I think I might be pregnant."

CHAPTER FIFTEEN

OVER THE PAST few years, marriage and babies had dramatically transformed the Malone world, passing through their playboy landscape like a fast-moving glacier, carving new patterns that were simultaneously very strange and very beautiful.

But one thing never changed. No matter what, Sunday afternoons belonged to the boat, the bay and the brothers.

Today, as the *MacGregor* sailboat skimmed across the choppy, blue-black bay, it held only Colby and Matt. Red had been elected to stay home with Nana Lina. Though they hoped she hadn't noticed, their grandmother hadn't been completely alone a single minute since the diagnosis.

Selfishly, Colby was glad it was just the two of them today. Having all three Malone brothers in the same place always brought out the comedian in someone. And the conversation he wanted to have was no joke.

He waited until they'd toyed an hour or so with the brisk fall breeze, finding angles to play with the sails so that the *MacGregor* flew over the water like a herring gull. They rarely talked while they sailed in earnest, focusing instead on the boat and the elements. Today they were sailing under main alone, about ten knots an hour, and concentration was crucial.

Eventually, the wind in their ears, the sun on their faces and the burn in their arms told them they'd left the kinks of daily life behind. Matt had the wheel, so Colby stood to reduce sail. They'd bought the roller reefing main last year, so it took only a few seconds.

Colby handed Matt the coffee thermos. November had blown into San Francisco with below-average temps, and they never drank beer in what they called "numb-nose" weather.

Matt cupped his mug in both hands, warming his fingers. He blew on the coffee, then took a drink. His eyes watched Colby over the rim, obviously aware that something was up.

But he undoubtedly assumed that Colby's tension was all Hayley-related. Colby screwed the cap on the thermos roughly and stowed it. How in hell was he going to get this conversation started?

And if he found it difficult to tell Matt about Marguerite, how much more impossible would it be to tell Hayley?

"So…" Matt leaned back and watched a thirty-two-footer showing off in the middle distance, his tone and posture both giving the impression that his question was an idle one. "Did things warm up in Sonoma after we left the other night?"

"Not much." Colby decided to cut right to the chase. "But that's not what's bothering me. It's not Hayley."

Matt's eyebrows twitched, the only sign that he was surprised—and maybe a little skeptical. "No?"

"No. It's much worse than that. It's Marguerite."

Matt pulled his head back an inch, incredulous. "Marguerite? The redhead from August?"

And suddenly, with that one sentence, Colby recognized how superficial and absurd his love life was, as if he saw with someone else's eyes.

Hayley's eyes.

But it was true. No one, including him, remembered his girlfriends except by hair color and month…as if they were nothing more than fold-out photos in the glossy tabloid of his life. Marguerite, an intelligent, talented woman, had been reduced to Miss August.

"Yes. Marguerite. She does in-house PR for her father's chain of liquor stores. Her IQ is higher than ours put together, and she's been on the planning and zoning board for the past five years."

Matt widened his eyes. "Sorry," he said with mild sarcasm. "Didn't mean to *objectify* her. You might possibly have neglected to mention all those impressive particulars. You know, back in August."

"Sorry." Colby knew it didn't improve things, to try to give Marguerite her due now. Now that it was far too late. "I'm just edgy, that's all."

"Edgy because…" Matt waited.

The wind tossed Colby's hair down onto his forehead, and he shoved it out of the way irritably. "Because she thinks she might be pregnant."

Whatever Colby had thought Matt might do upon hearing that announcement, it didn't happen. He didn't recoil or gasp or drop his coffee. His mouth didn't fall open, or spit out a four-letter expletive.

And that's how Colby knew how bad his news was. It was so bad, so hopeless and wretched and raw, that no reaction in the world could do it justice.

His brother might as well have turned to stone.

"Say something, damn it." Colby tossed his cooling coffee into the bay with one vicious jerk. "Tell me I'm a fool, a bastard, an arrogant, reckless chump who's had it coming for a long, long time."

Matt shrugged, finally appearing to recover his wits. "Wouldn't that be a waste of breath? Sounds as if you've already called yourself every name I could possibly think of."

His voice was calm, but laced with a subtle sympathy that made Colby's flesh crawl. It was the voice you used at the bedside of a dying aunt.

His eyes, resting on Colby's face, looked that way, too. "When did you find out?"

"The other night. She called. She's been calling for days."

Matt nodded. "You said she *thinks* she's pregnant. What does that mean? These days, don't they sell tests that can tell you for sure…like thirty seconds after you have sex?"

"I asked her that. She just repeats that she's pretty sure she's pregnant. Whatever that means. She doesn't seem a lot happier about it than I am."

"What does she want you to do?"

Colby frowned. "If she is pregnant, she's keeping it."

"Yeah, but after that. I mean, what does she see as the best-case scenario? Is she looking for money? Or is she looking for a white dress and a priest?"

"I don't know. We…we didn't get into those details yet. She was upset, and she said she wanted to wait until after she'd seen the doctor."

"Which is?"

"Tomorrow."

"Great. Nana Lina's surgery, and this kind of mess, all in the same day." Matt tapped his fingers pensively against the wooden wheel for a few minutes, beating out a complex pattern that only he could understand. Finally, he looked up.

"I know you don't fool around with stuff like this," he said. "Not after…"

"No. I damn sure don't."

Even back when he was eighteen, he'd used condoms. But a few times, with Hayley, when he'd wanted her so bad it was like torture, and there hadn't been enough little silver packets, or enough time to buy more or enough patience to wait, he'd told her—told himself—that pulling out would work.

She'd been nervous. But he'd promised her that it was a sure thing. It wasn't really a risk, not as long as he was careful, not as long as he knew what he was doing. He had kissed her and touched her and begged her, until she had said yes.

Three, four, five times, maybe, in all. But often enough to bring disaster raining down on both of them.

So no. He never fooled around with that kind of thing anymore. Even if a woman was on five different kinds of birth control, his condoms were fresh, plentiful and always at hand. Besides, he'd never wanted anyone that much, not after Hayley. If the time wasn't right, then next time was always soon enough. Waiting was no big deal.

"So, if you are as careful as I suspect you are, isn't there a possibility it's—"

"Not mine?" Colby laughed, the bitter sound ripped

out of his mouth by the cold wind. "You know, for some reason I don't feel inclined to work that angle."

"No. Of course not." Matt shook his head so faintly he probably didn't even know he was doing it. "And the timing. Could it be any worse? If Hayley found out…"

And there it was, dropped like a bomb in the boat. The heart of the matter.

He'd had several sleepless nights to think about it. And he'd decided that, by itself, Marguerite's news was not the end of the world. If she were going to have his baby, they could find a way to deal with it. She'd be a good mother, and he'd always intended to be a father. Someday.

In spite of his reputation as a playboy, he didn't date women unless he respected them on some level. Why spend even a month with a woman who was stupid, or unkind or immoral?

So, though he could feel sorry for himself and mourn the loss of the perfect family he'd always dreamed about, he would survive. Plenty of men had found themselves in this situation, and life went on. Joint-custody arrangements were invented for this very scenario.

But Hayley.

"What if she did find out?" Matt sighed, as if the prospect were almost too much to think about. "What do you think she'd say?"

The clouds had parted, and the sun hit the choppy waves like a thousand photographer's flashbulbs going off at once. Colby squinted his eyes against the intensity of the sparks.

"That's easy," he replied flatly. "I think she'd say goodbye."

HAYLEY'S MONDAY STARTED PERFECTLY, a little jewel of a morning in which everything went right. It had rained at dawn, but then the clouds blew away, and the sunshine bathed everything in honey.

After a couple of nights at the hotel, she'd come back here Saturday. She'd told the Eliots about Greg, and they'd promised to keep an eye out. She'd also told the police, who had offered to drive by every hour or so, just to double-check.

She'd done fine. When she went to bed, she'd kept all the lights on, and her dad's baseball bat propped against the nightstand. But the night had been quiet. She'd slept like a baby and awakened feeling strong, as if she could handle anything.

Maybe it was because the house was looking so good. The estate-sale agent had removed half of the furniture, and she'd donated some to charity. Only the best pieces, the things she thought she and Genevieve might use, were left. The rooms didn't look, or smell, like her father anymore.

Best of all, now that it was down to its bare bones, the lovely lines of the architecture were visible, and she realized the house actually had a lot of charm. She could finally imagine someone buying it, and living here, maybe raising a family and banishing all the old ghosts forever.

She made coffee and toast with fresh local jelly, one of the jars her old friend Merry Evans had brought her when she visited the other day. She'd have to remember to get Merry's new address, so that she could write her when she got back to Florida. She didn't intend to let another seventeen years ago by without keeping in touch with her rediscovered friends.

For the past couple of hours, she'd been sorting the last boxes of her old mementos, carrying them up one at a time from basement storage, so that she could sit in the living room, even though there were no chairs left. She liked to look up and see the sun picking out rain diamonds on the vines.

Three big boxes finished, and no heartaches had emerged to spoil the morning yet. The ones she'd chosen were from pre-Colby days—horseback-riding ribbons, and spelling-bee medals, baby teeth in jewelry boxes and a note from Gen in baby handwriting that said "I luv u halz."

She smiled, tucking the note into the small pile of keepers. Yes, she could do this, and she was going to be fine. She began to hum one of her mother's old songs.

And then the mail came.

The postman knocked, which was unusual. She glanced at her watch—only about five minutes to eleven. He was hours earlier than usual. Plus, the door had a slot, and usually he just stuffed the few flyers and bills through, letting them puddle on the floor.

"Hi," he said when she opened the door. He held out a clipboard. "I need you to sign for this one."

She was curious, but nothing more. It wasn't until she sat down on the newly cleaned blond wood floor and opened the letter that she realized who it was from.

Abruptly, her heart began to beat so fast she couldn't quite breathe. The return address was College Park, Florida. Sender's name: Anna Tichner.

Hayley's fingers shook as she yanked the letter out

of its packaging. As she read the words, a wave of ice passed through her, and her whole body began to shake. The letters swam as her eyes burned, and everything fogged. She saw only bits of sentences....

But she saw enough to know.

Anna Tichner had changed her mind. She wanted to keep her baby.

She'd been feeling twinges of doubt ever since she first felt the baby move, she wrote. But the episode in the hospital last week had clinched it. When she faced the possibility of losing the baby to a miscarriage, she'd finally understood. She was sorry, so very, very sorry. But she just couldn't give her baby up. Not ever. Not even to Hayley.

Hayley heard an anguished sound that must have come from her own lips. The letter fell onto the floor.

She stared at it a minute, as if it were a living, dangerous thing. Then she climbed to her feet. She had to get away from it.

For a mindless time, she paced the half-empty rooms, trying to make her muscles stop shaking. At first, the strange, fluttering things that threw themselves at the walls of her brain were hardly even words. They were just half-born bits of pain, and anger and denial.

No. No. Anna couldn't do this. They had signed a contract. It wasn't fair. It wasn't legal. It wasn't fair, it wasn't fair, it wasn't fair....

She rushed to the sink, suddenly nauseated, as if her stomach might reject the toast she'd eaten earlier. But when she bent over, nothing happened. She turned on the water, as cold as she could stand, and splashed it on her face.

She wanted to cry, sure that if she didn't, the pain would keep swelling inside her until something...her heart...exploded. But tears wouldn't come.

The tap water rolled down her cheeks, pooled on her chin and dripped into the empty sink. But she couldn't cry.

Gradually, the hot edge of the pain receded. Her blood calmed and, inch by inch, her body seemed to belong to her again. She could even feel her mind clearing, a little. Maybe she should call Gen. Maybe, if she had someone to talk to, she would stop feeling as if she were living inside a horror film.

But that was wrong, too. She couldn't call Gen now, when she was so fractured, so broken. Gen would be terrified—she'd never seen her big sister so undone, not since...

She took a deep breath. There was no one to turn to. No one but herself. Somehow, she had to face this and be strong.

She grabbed a paper towel from the dispenser, rubbed it hard over her face to get the blood flowing and reached out to touch the back of the kitchen stool for balance.

She glanced at the flower-shaped clock that still hung over the refrigerator, and then double-checked her watch. Was it possible that only about five minutes had elapsed since the postman arrived at the door? Surely it took more than five minutes to hollow out a human being, so that everything inside her, every hope and dream and plan and wish, was gone.

And yet…

She sat quietly for a long, long time, trying to sort through the pain, down to the truth. As lost and numb and brokenhearted as she felt right now, could she honestly say she was completely shocked? Hadn't the idea of adopting Anna Tichner's baby always felt just a little bit too good to be true?

How many times had she stopped herself from saying the words *my baby?* It had always sounded wrong. Unlucky, as if taking it for granted would jinx it.

Maybe, from somewhere deep inside, the girl she used to be had tried to tell her not to be overly confident. Giving up the child that had grown inside you wasn't easy, even when you were young and terrified and alone.

If Hayley herself had been given a choice, she would never have let anyone take her baby away. It had required force, and brutality and pain…and even then her body had held on as long as it could. Years later, she still sometimes woke in the night, her hand on her flat stomach, trying to keep the baby from leaving her.

I'm sorry, so very, very sorry…

Hayley pictured the letter, still lying on the floor. Anna's childish scrawl was ragged with distress. The unhappy girl had no doubt sensed how much this letter would hurt the woman who received it. But she had somehow found the courage to speak the truth. She loved her child, and she wanted to be a mother.

"Good for you, Anna," Hayley whispered. *Good for you.*

And then, finally, her tears began to flow. She lowered her head to the cool granite countertop, and she cried. After seventeen years of being strong, she was ready to feel the pain.

She wept for Anna, and Elena, for her own seventeen-year-old self and the baby who never lived. She cried for her mother, for Gen's lost childhood and for the vineyard that no one loved. She cried for Colby, and for every beautiful, nameless thing that had ever slipped through her fingers because she was afraid to reach out and clasp it tightly.

And suddenly, as if her tears had been prayers, he was there, knocking at the back door. Perhaps he'd been knocking a long time, and she hadn't been aware. He was practically pounding by the time she heard him, using the heel of his fist. His face was drawn, clearly worried, watching her through the glass.

She went to the door, not even bothering to wipe the tears from her cheeks. She twisted the lock, and pulled the door open quickly. He surged in, taking her in his arms as if that were the most natural reaction in the world.

"What's wrong?" He held her close. "Hayley, what's wrong?"

She shook her head, breathing in the scent of him, the clean fragrance of leather car seats, minty shaving cream and honey. He had always smelled like honey.

"Is it Valmont? Has he been here?" Colby's arms were tight around her, and she heard the protective vehemence in his voice.

"No," she said, shaking her head again, loving the soft, sensual slide of broadcloth against her cheek. "No, he hasn't come. It isn't Greg."

His heavy, relieved exhale feathered her hair, which she hadn't pulled back this morning. He touched the crown of her head with his lips. "What is it, then, sweetheart? Why are you crying?"

"Because—"

She buried her face in his chest again without finishing the thought. She didn't want to talk about it. She didn't want to discuss and analyze and pin this feeling down with words. She wanted, for the first time in seventeen years, to simply listen to her heart. She wanted, for once, to reach out and take what she wanted, before it, too, slipped through her fingers.

And what she wanted was Colby. Colby could fill this hollow place inside her.

She lifted her face. She probably looked horrible, with swollen eyes and streaked face, but she didn't care. "I don't want to talk about it, Colby. I don't want to talk about anything."

His eyes darkened. "What do you want, then?"

"I want you to hold me. I want you to make love to me. Just this once. I want to have that memory, to take with me when I leave."

His eyes went almost black, and she remembered that, too. It was the look that meant he was about to burn up with desire. His arms tightened.

"Hayley," he began. "We should—"

"No." She put her fingers over his mouth, though the heat of him almost scalded her. "Please. I don't want to talk, or even think."

"I can't—I can't stay," he said. "My grandmother is having surgery this afternoon. If we—" He looked miserable. "I only have a couple of hours before I have to leave."

"If a couple of hours is all you have, I'll take it. If you don't want me, Colby, then just go. But if you do—"

"Don't *want* you?" He laughed, a dark and feverish sound. "Don't *want* you?"

He shifted his hands, and with one strong movement lifted her from the ground. Instinctively, she wrapped her legs around his back, just as he lowered his harsh, passionate face to hers. When he kissed her, his hot lips hard and probing, every muscle in her body went momentarily limp. Only his hands, one firmly behind her head, and one pressed against her buttocks, saved her from falling.

"Don't *want* you," he muttered one more time, half laughing, against her mouth. "Damn it, Hayley. How could you be so wrong?"

And then, as if she weighed no more than a child, he moved into the foyer and started up the stairs. Relief spread through her veins, followed by a trail of fiery desire.

She was finally in Colby Malone's arms again. She let her head fall against his shoulder and shut her swollen eyes. Two hours was such a short time.

But it was something. And after seventeen years of *nothing,* that was enough.

CHAPTER SIXTEEN

COLBY HAD FORGOTTEN that the only bed left in the house was the tiny twin he and Red had transferred into her father's room the day of the Eliots' barn fire.

The door stood half open, and he elbowed through it roughly, too impatient to care about noise or scuff marks on the wall. The narrow bed was practically the only piece of furniture in the large, echoing room. It looked like an altar, covered in a simple white cloth, bathed in light from the large windows that overlooked the vineyard.

He laid her on it gently, trying to believe this was really happening. With her gold-and-silver curls spread out on the pillow, and her blue eyes gazing up at him with all that smoldering, desperately banked fire, she looked like the recurring dream that had tormented him half his life.

Was it possible that this time she was real? Or would she start to dissolve beneath his fingers, disappearing in trails of light, like the embers of fireworks? Would he wake up at home, bathed in sweat, his body hard and helpless?

"Say something," he whispered as he knelt between her legs, looking down at her. "I need to be sure you're really here."

Her lips were parted, her breath coming shallowly.

She touched the buckle of his belt, then let her fingers slide down the denim of his jeans, tracing the rigid length of him. "I'm really here," she said.

He groaned, saying a quick prayer that he would, in the end, be able to control himself. When she asked him to make love to her, he had known he should simply say no. Marguerite had not called—she hadn't lifted that sword from his head. He had thought about it, remembered the stringent precautions he always, always took. He'd run the dates in his head a thousand times. It would sound to anyone else like a classic male cop-out, but the truth was he honestly believed there was almost no chance Marguerite could possibly be carrying his child.

But *almost no chance* wasn't the same as no chance at all. If Hayley knew…

She would never forgive him for taking the same life-changing risk with her—not when he still hadn't paid in full for the risks he'd already taken with another woman. She would feel exploited, endangered—and if one condom could fail, why couldn't two condoms fail? Could he possibly risk putting her in a situation like that? A nightmare scenario in which not one, but *two* of Colby Malone's cheap thrills ended up pregnant at the same time?

So he'd sworn to himself that, if he carried her up these stairs, it would be only for the opportunity to give her pleasure. He would not take what she offered, so innocently. He would only give.

But he hadn't quite imagined the pain…

He slowly unbuttoned her soft blue shirt, and when she lifted up on her elbows to let the cotton slide back, her breasts touched his chest, and he nearly lost himself again.

The lacy white bra hooked in front, and he peeled it away urgently. Her breasts… Oh, he had always loved her breasts. Firm white swells with full, pink thrusting tips. He got stuck there for countless minutes, tasting her, remembering what she loved, what coaxed the small hungry sounds from her swollen lips.

He sucked softly, pulling her into the darkness of his mouth while she kneaded his head and shifted her hips, as if her nipples were connected by some invisible golden thread to the spot between her legs.

She kept reaching up, trying to remove his clothes, too, and he grew so long and hard that with every single brush of her fingers, he feared he might give in. But somehow he held on. He'd set the limits. He knew what they were, and for once in his godforsaken, spoiled playboy life, he was going to stay within them.

Somehow he got all her clothing off, even the lacy wisp of cloth between her legs, and when he bent his head to kiss her smooth thighs, her searching hands dropped weakly at her sides.

He had never made love to her in the daylight before, and for a moment he couldn't move, lost in the awe of seeing her there, utterly naked and beautiful, open to him, unashamed, every inch of her pale, slim body washed in sunlight.

She was the same, she was the dream, she was Hayley. And yet, in some mysterious way, she was also new, more womanly, more exciting.

He'd made love to many women since the last time he touched Hayley Watson. Back then, he'd been a selfish boy who cared more for his own pleasure than for hers. He longed to show her how different he was now.

And yet, for a terrifying moment, it was as if he knew nothing at all. He had made love to many women, yes…

But he had never made love to a woman he loved.

She took his hand and guided it to the soft golden curls between her legs. "It's all right," she said, shutting her eyes as his flesh met hers. "It's me, Colby. It's still me."

His fingers settled against her, taking a minute to relearn the contours of her secret places, the rhythm of the heated pulse that beat against his fingertips.

The subtle smell of roses floated up as she shifted on the sheets. Her hips rotated delicately, and suddenly everything was clear again.

Oh, yes. Yes. His hands, his heart, his entire body remembered what she wanted.

She moaned softly, as his fingers began to move. He kept them moving, circling and searching, until he could tell she was ready to fall. She had begun to shift her head on the pillow, a restless, panting signal that she wanted to wait for him, but wasn't sure she could.

His own body was throbbing, so swollen against the denim of his jeans that every movement was pain. He ignored it. He had to ignore it. This moment wasn't about him. This moment was about what she needed.

He could never make up for all those nights he'd spilled himself inside her carelessly, telling himself he'd take care of her next time, he had to get home, it was late, she was out after curfew anyhow, and there would be hell to pay if they lingered.

But he was going to try.

"No, wait…" Once more, she touched her hand to his belt, trying to fumble it open, but he gently took it away and held it against the sheet.

Then he lowered his head and took the sensitive bud of her between his lips. She fell back against the pillow with a low whimper, forgetting about his belt, clearly no longer really aware of anything but the rhythmic tug and release of his mouth.

He lifted her legs, one at a time, and rested them across his shoulders, changing her position a mere fraction of an inch. From here, he was in total control, able to adjust the pressure and the pace so minutely that he could lead her to the ultimate edge of pleasure, and keep her there forever.

For the first few seconds, he felt her trying to restrain herself, but that couldn't last. Soon she was lost, and she moaned mindlessly, shifting, her legs tightening desperately against his back. She pressed herself against him, tilting her hips at a ruthless angle, blindly seeking release.

The tiny bud under his tongue kept hardening, and swelling, until he knew she must be half-mad with the pressure. He backed off just the least little bit, giving her a second to breathe. He licked once, then once more, to be sure she stayed on the edge, and he felt a cascade of shivers run down her legs, all the way to her toes.

And then he closed in again, this time in earnest. She cried out, the sound echoing in the empty room, and her fingers kneaded themselves into his hair. Her body was a fiery liquid beneath his lips.

"Please," she breathed. Then, increasing the pressure, he gave her what she needed.

Time stopped. She lifted, crying out, and he took her hands with his and clung to her as she fell…desperate and sweating and burning in one combined fire. In a surge of wonder he'd never experienced before, he had the strange sensation that he was her body, and she was his, and they were no longer two people, no longer separate, no longer alone.

He couldn't tell which of the waves of scalding pleasure came from her, and which were some kind of mystical answer from his own body. When she peaked and shuddered, and the tension finally began to drain out of her, he felt it, too.

A minute later, he rose, kissed her lips and then fell helplessly to the side, as drained as if he, too, had experienced a physical climax. Even as their breath slowed, the aftershocks kept coming, like ripples spreading out across an ocean.

It seemed to last forever. He wanted to speak, but he didn't have the energy to move his lips. What had happened to him? He was still hard, still swollen and unsatisfied, and yet he felt paralyzed with pleasure, weak with contentment.

She turned her face to him, her eyes still a little glazed, but confused. "Colby," she said softly. "What about you?"

He shook his head. "This time, it's not about me," he said. "This time, it's about you."

"But—" She frowned. "Oh. You couldn't have guessed, of course. You didn't bring… You don't have a condom?"

He smiled. Of course he had a condom. He always, always had a condom. But he didn't tell her that. He just turned her gently and tucked her up against him, her fairy-bud shoulder blades against his chest.

"I have everything I need," he said, his breath shimmering the fine curls at the base of her neck.

"But—" She obviously felt she should argue, but her body was betraying her, going limp with exhausted satisfaction. He wrapped his arms around her, knowing he, too, was about to sink into oblivion. He wanted to let his body drink her in as he slept.

"I have everything I need," he repeated.

And suddenly, as he slipped into unconsciousness, he knew it was true. This was where he belonged. The days of pretending all women were interchangeable playthings, no one more important than the next, no one powerful enough to hurt him, were gone forever.

There was something he should remember…some thorn lurking here…some trouble yet to be faced. But he was drifting, he was dreaming, and he couldn't recall what it was.

All he knew for certain was that he would never again make love to anyone else. It was Hayley… Hayley's hair between his fingers, Hayley's lips between his teeth…Hayley's body closing around him…

Or no one.

WHEN SHE WOKE, HE was gone.

Of course he was. He had told her he could give her only two hours. His grandmother was having surgery.

She was still naked. Her loose hair tickled her back and her breasts. Her whole body still felt sensitive and slightly aroused from the ferocity of his lovemaking. She yawned, and stretched, aware of all the newly awakened and raw spots.

Wrapping the sheet around herself, she stood and walked to the window overlooking the vineyard. It was late afternoon—she must have slept for hours.

The vines looked as if they'd been painted gold. A curl of silver smoke rose from the Eliots' house, and over by the overlook, some Ellenton-Barnes employee was walking the rows of pinot, probably checking to see if any clusters had been left behind by the pickers.

She'd expected to feel desolate, with Colby gone, the house echoing and empty and Anna's letter still lying, discarded, on the living-room floor.

She did feel a little weak. Confused on some very profound level, as if she lived in a changed world, and hadn't yet figured out her place. And vulnerable, like a creature that had lost its shell, and could be easily hurt.

Yet, while these feelings were frightening, they weren't entirely unpleasant. Though it seemed ridiculous to say so, in the strangest way, she felt…

As if she had been reborn.

She shut her eyes, overwhelmed. Reborn? How could that be?

It was partly Colby. And the ecstasy of lying there with him. Being in his arms again was the second chance she'd always dreamed of. He had shown her physical bliss like nothing she'd ever experienced. The glow of that wouldn't fade soon. As memories went, it was going to be an endless treasure.

As she gazed down on the bucolic charm of the vineyard she'd always loved so dearly, she suddenly realized why her world seemed so new and full of possibilities. This amazing sense of rebirth wasn't merely a sexual thing. It went far deeper than that.

When Anna Tichner decided she couldn't give her baby up for adoption, she had essentially chosen the escape clause that had always been written into their contract. She'd always had ninety days after the birth of the baby to change her mind.

And now that she had, the entire contract was null and void.

Including the part that said Hayley Watson was required to live in Florida.

It took away Hayley's dream of having a baby. But it also meant that she was free.

She shivered, and hugged the cotton sheet tighter around her shoulders.

It meant that if she decided she didn't want to sell Foggy Valley, she didn't have to. It meant that she could stay.

NANA LINA'S SURGERY had been scheduled for 3:00 p.m. Colby had hoped to be at the hospital by two, but a five-car pileup on the bay bridge blocked his way. By the time he arrived, she was being wheeled in. She was already groggy, and not making a lot of sense.

When she spied him by the gurney, she raised one finger and pointed at him sternly. "I've got something to say to you, Colby Malone. I'm a little busy now, but I expect you to present yourself the minute I wake up."

Behind him, Red and Matt had chuckled. They didn't actually singsong the words, as they used to do as kids—"Colby is in trou-ble"—but they might as well